The Lost Scrolls of Andalusia

Young Adult Fiction: Religious – Muslim, Volume 2

Amina Zahra

Published by Arcane Horizons Publishing, 2024.

THE LOST SCROLLS OF ANDALUSIA

First edition. December 7, 2024.

ISBN: 979-8230422747

Written by Amina Zahra.

Table of Contents

To the seekers of truth,

who walk the path of knowledge with faith as their guide.

May these words serve as a reminder of the rich legacy left by those
who came before us, and may their wisdom light your way forward.

For my family, whose love and support are my constant strength, and
for every soul who strives for excellence in both faith and action—

this book is for you.

Chapter 1: The Discovery – A Forgotten Legacy

———

The Andalusian sun hung low in the sky, casting golden light over the city of Cordoba. Idris, a nineteen-year-old university student studying Islamic history, stood at the entrance of the *Mezquita-Catedral*, lost in thought. This visit was meant to be the highlight of his summer trip with his family, but he couldn't shake the nagging feeling that this place held more than just its beautiful architecture and historical significance.

Since his childhood, Idris had been fascinated by Andalusia. His father, a history professor, had often recounted tales of the Golden Age of Islam, when Muslim scholars in the Iberian Peninsula were at the forefront of knowledge, art, and science. Andalusia was the place where Ibn Rushd had written his philosophical treatises and where Ibn Firnas had dreamt of flight. It was a land of poets, scholars, and innovators. But over time, that legacy had been lost, buried under centuries of conflict and conquest.

Now, standing in the courtyard of the *Mezquita-Catedral*, Idris felt a deep sense of connection to the past, as though the stories of Islamic Andalusia were not mere historical anecdotes, but living memories waiting to be uncovered.

Idris' family had spread out to explore different sections of the mosque, each eager to experience its grandeur in their own way. He had stayed behind, his mind wandering as he tried to imagine what it must have been like to live during the height of Islamic rule here—when this mosque had been filled with scholars reciting the Qur'an, discussing mathematics, and engaging in philosophical debates.

He walked slowly, his eyes tracing the intricate patterns carved into the pillars and arches, marveling at the harmony between Islamic and Gothic architectural elements. The contrast between the mosque's original Islamic design and the Christian modifications made after the Reconquista intrigued him. It was a symbol of history's layers, of civilizations that had risen and fallen over time.

As he wandered, something unusual caught his eye. Beyond a set of wooden barriers that seemed to be set up for restoration work, there was a small, shadowy alcove. The door to the alcove was slightly ajar, and from where Idris stood, it looked as though no one had entered it for years.

A rush of curiosity surged through him. He looked around quickly, and seeing that no one was watching, he slipped past the barrier and into the alcove. The air was cool and thick with the smell of dust and old stone. The narrow hallway led him deeper into the bowels of the mosque, away from the tourists and into an untouched part of the ancient structure.

The hallway eventually opened into a small room, dimly lit by shafts of sunlight streaming through a high window. In the corner of the room, half-covered by debris and dirt, was an old wooden chest. Idris' heart skipped a beat. The chest looked ancient, its wood darkened by age, and the intricate carvings on its surface suggested it was from a time long past.

He approached the chest cautiously, his hands trembling with anticipation. His mind raced as he imagined what could be inside. A thousand possibilities flashed before him—old relics, forgotten manuscripts, or even mundane tools left behind by workers centuries ago. But something told him that this chest held more than just forgotten remnants of a bygone era.

With a deep breath, Idris knelt beside the chest and carefully wiped away the dust. The carvings on the lid were unmistakably Islamic—beautifully rendered Arabic script and geometric patterns, symbols of a time when Andalusia had been a center of learning and culture. The inscription read: *"Al-Hikmah min Allah"* —*"Wisdom is from Allah."*

Idris paused for a moment, his heart racing. Could this chest have belonged to a scholar from that golden era? His hands shook slightly as he slowly lifted the lid.

Inside, wrapped in faded cloth, were several scrolls. The parchment was yellowed and fragile, the ink faded but still legible in places. Idris reached out and carefully unwrapped the first scroll. His breath caught in his throat as he realized what he was holding.

The scroll was written in classical Arabic, and though Idris wasn't fluent, his years of studying Islamic history allowed him to recognize some of the words. He saw terms like *hikmah* (wisdom), *ilm* (knowledge), and *iman* (faith). The handwriting was precise, elegant, and clearly the work of a scholar. This was no ordinary text—this was something far more significant.

As he carefully unfurled more of the scroll, he found references to Andalusian scholars, passages discussing philosophical ideas, and even notes on scientific advancements in astronomy and medicine. These were not just random musings; these scrolls were the writings of scholars from a time when Andalusia had been a beacon of knowledge for the entire world. The discovery felt overwhelming.

Idris' pulse quickened. He had come here to learn more about Islamic history, but he had never imagined that he would find something like this. These scrolls—these fragile, ancient pieces of parchment—held the wisdom of a time long gone, a time when Islamic civilization had been at the forefront of intellectual and scientific progress.

He gently placed the scroll back in the chest, his mind spinning with questions. Who had written these scrolls? Why had they been hidden here, in this forgotten corner of the mosque? And most importantly, what secrets did they hold about the golden era of Andalusia?

Idris knew that he had stumbled upon something incredibly important, something that could potentially change his understanding of Islamic history. But this was only the beginning. The scrolls were written in a form of Arabic that would take time to fully decipher, and Idris knew he would need help from scholars who specialized in this period of history. But that didn't discourage him—if anything, it fueled his determination.

The weight of the discovery settled over him, and he felt a deep sense of responsibility. These scrolls were not just relics of the past; they were keys to understanding the present. The knowledge they contained had been lost to time, buried under centuries of conflict and neglect. But now, they had a chance to resurface, to shed light on a forgotten legacy and inspire future generations.

As Idris carefully closed the chest and stood up, his mind raced with possibilities. How could he share this knowledge with others? What impact could it have on the modern Muslim world, which often seemed disconnected from its rich intellectual and spiritual heritage?

The questions swirled in his mind as he made his way back through the hallway and out into the bright Andalusian afternoon. His family was still wandering through the mosque, unaware of the incredible discovery Idris had just made. But as he rejoined them, he couldn't help but feel that something had shifted within him.

This journey to Andalusia had started as a simple family trip, but it had transformed into something far greater. Idris had uncovered a forgotten legacy, one that would shape not only his understanding of history but his faith and his future.

Reflection: How Can the Knowledge of the Past Shape the Faith and Understanding of Future Generations?

AS IDRIS LEFT THE MOSQUE, his thoughts turned to the question that had begun to form in his mind: how could the knowledge of the past shape the future of the Muslim community? The discovery of the scrolls had ignited a passion within him to reconnect with the rich intellectual tradition of Islam, a tradition that had been marginalized and forgotten by many.

The scholars of Andalusia had once been leaders in fields like science, philosophy, medicine, and theology. They had exemplified the Qur'anic call to seek knowledge, and their contributions had shaped the course of history. But over time, that knowledge had been lost or overshadowed by the challenges of colonialism, modernity, and globalization.

Idris realized that by uncovering these scrolls, he had an opportunity—perhaps even a responsibility—to reignite that spirit of inquiry and intellectual curiosity in today's generation. The lessons of the past were not just historical footnotes; they were living examples of how faith and reason could coexist, how spiritual and intellectual pursuits could enrich one another.

As he thought about the challenges facing the modern Muslim world—struggles with identity, faith, and a sense of purpose—he wondered if reconnecting with the wisdom of Andalusia could provide answers. The teachings of those ancient scholars, preserved in the fragile scrolls, had the potential to inspire a new generation of Muslims to seek knowledge, to question, and to strive for excellence in both faith and intellect.

The journey ahead would be long, and the work would be challenging, but Idris felt ready. The legacy of Andalusia was not lost—it was waiting to be rediscovered, waiting to shine its light once more.

And Idris was determined to be the one to carry that light forward.

Chapter 2: The Scholars of Andalusia – Seeking Knowledge

The scrolls lay unfurled on the wooden table in front of Idris, their delicate parchment illuminated by the soft glow of the desk lamp. His eyes scanned the ancient Arabic script, trying to decipher the words written centuries ago. The intricate calligraphy made it difficult to read, but Idris was determined. He had been working on the translation for several days now, making slow but steady progress. Each word felt like a key, unlocking a treasure trove of knowledge that had been hidden for generations.

The weight of the discovery was not lost on him. These scrolls—these forgotten manuscripts—contained the writings of scholars who had lived during the Golden Age of Andalusia, a period of Islamic history when knowledge was revered as a form of worship. The scholars of that era had not only preserved the wisdom of ancient civilizations but had also made groundbreaking contributions to fields such as science, philosophy, medicine, and theology. For them, the pursuit of knowledge was more than just an intellectual exercise—it was a spiritual endeavor, a means of drawing closer to Allah.

As Idris translated the scrolls, he found himself immersed in the world of these scholars, their words transporting him to a time when learning was celebrated as a divine act. The more he read, the more he realized that the scholars of Andalusia had understood something profound: that knowledge, when pursued with sincerity and humility, was a pathway to both personal growth and spiritual enlightenment.

The Pursuit of Knowledge as a Form of Worship

ONE OF THE FIRST PASSAGES Idris translated spoke directly to the relationship between knowledge and faith. The scroll quoted a well-known hadith of the Prophet Muhammad (PBUH):

"Seeking knowledge is an obligation upon every Muslim."

(Sunan Ibn Majah)

Idris had heard this hadith many times before, but seeing it written in the scroll, in the elegant script of a scholar from centuries past, gave it new meaning. The scholars of Andalusia had taken this hadith to heart, viewing the pursuit of knowledge as an essential aspect of their faith. They believed that by seeking knowledge, they were fulfilling a divine command, one that brought them closer to Allah and deepened their understanding of His creation.

The scrolls revealed that the scholars of Andalusia had a holistic view of knowledge. They did not see a divide between religious and secular learning; instead, they believed that all knowledge was interconnected and that understanding the natural world was a means of glorifying the Creator. This was a concept Idris found deeply inspiring. In today's world, knowledge was often compartmentalized, with religion and science treated as separate, sometimes even opposing, fields. But the scholars of Andalusia had bridged this gap, seeing no contradiction between their faith and their intellectual pursuits.

As Idris continued his translation, he came across another passage that elaborated on this idea. The scholar who had written the scroll—likely an Andalusian philosopher or theologian—had penned the following reflection:

"Knowledge is the light that illuminates the soul, guiding it toward the recognition of Allah's majesty. In the study of the heavens and the earth, in the exploration of the human mind and heart, we find the signs of Allah's presence. Every discovery, every truth, leads us back to the One who created all things."

These words resonated deeply with Idris. The scholar was expressing a truth that had been central to the intellectual culture of Andalusia: that the pursuit of knowledge was a form of worship, a way of drawing closer to Allah by understanding His creation. Whether they were studying the stars, developing medical treatments, or debating philosophical ideas, the scholars of Andalusia believed that their work was an act of devotion.

Idris paused for a moment, reflecting on his own approach to learning. As a university student, he had always enjoyed studying history and philosophy, but he had never thought of his academic pursuits as a form of worship. Now, he began to see things differently. The Qur'an repeatedly called on believers to reflect on the natural world and to seek knowledge as a way of recognizing Allah's greatness. Idris realized that every piece of knowledge, every truth he uncovered, was an opportunity to deepen his faith and strengthen his connection to Allah.

One of the verses that came to his mind was from *Surah Al-Mulk:*

"Do they not look at the sky above them—how We have built it and made it beautiful and free of flaws?"

(Qur'an 67:3)

This verse was a reminder that the natural world was full of signs pointing to Allah's existence. By studying these signs, by seeking to understand the world in all its complexity, believers were not only gaining intellectual insight—they were also engaging in an act of worship. Idris felt a sense of awe as he thought about this. The pursuit of knowledge was not just about accumulating facts or passing exams—it was about connecting with something far greater.

The Scholars of Andalusia: Bridging Science, Philosophy, and Faith

AS IDRIS DELVED DEEPER into the scrolls, he learned more about the scholars who had written them. These were men and women who had lived in a time when Andalusia was a center of learning, a place where scholars from different religious and cultural backgrounds came together to share ideas and advance knowledge. The scrolls mentioned several names that Idris recognized from his studies—figures like Ibn Rushd (Averroes), a philosopher and jurist, and Ibn al-Zahrawi (Abulcasis), a pioneering surgeon. These scholars had made significant contributions to fields ranging from medicine and astronomy to philosophy and theology, all while remaining deeply rooted in their Islamic faith.

What struck Idris most was how these scholars had managed to bridge the gap between science, philosophy, and religion. In modern times, these fields were often seen as distinct or even conflicting, but in Andalusia, they were viewed as complementary. The scholars believed that by studying the natural world and engaging in philosophical inquiry, they were fulfilling their religious duty to seek knowledge and understand Allah's creation.

One of the scrolls contained a passage written by an Andalusian philosopher who had been deeply influenced by the works of both Aristotle and Islamic theology. The passage read:

"Philosophy is not an enemy of faith, nor is science a threat to belief. Rather, they are tools by which we come to know the world that Allah has created. Through reason, we seek to understand the order and harmony of the universe, and through revelation, we learn of the purpose behind it. Together, they lead us to the truth."

Idris found this perspective fascinating. In a time when many people saw science and religion as being in conflict, the scholars of Andalusia had embraced both, seeing them as two sides of the same coin. For them, the pursuit of knowledge was not about choosing between faith and reason—it was about using both to arrive at a deeper understanding of the world and their place in it.

This holistic approach to knowledge was something Idris admired. It reminded him of how the Qur'an encouraged believers to use both their intellect and their faith to seek the truth. In *Surah Al-Baqarah*, Allah says:

"He grants wisdom to whom He wills, and whoever has been granted wisdom has certainly been given much good. But none will remember except those of understanding."

(Qur'an 2:269)

This verse highlighted the importance of wisdom, a gift that could only be attained through the pursuit of knowledge. The scholars of Andalusia had understood this well, and their contributions had shaped not only the intellectual landscape of their time but also the development of knowledge in the centuries that followed.

Idris continued translating the scrolls, his mind racing with thoughts about how the lessons of the past could be applied to the present. The scholars of Andalusia had valued knowledge as a form of worship, and they had sought to bridge the gap between science, philosophy, and religion. Their work had been driven by a deep sense of purpose, a belief that understanding the world around them was a way of honoring Allah's creation.

The Legacy of Andalusian Scholarship

AS IDRIS LEARNED MORE about the scholars of Andalusia, he couldn't help but feel a sense of awe at the legacy they had left behind. These were men and women who had lived in a time of intellectual flourishing, when the pursuit of knowledge was seen as a noble and sacred endeavor. They had built libraries, founded universities, and written works that would influence generations of scholars to come. Their contributions to fields such as medicine, astronomy, philosophy, and theology had shaped the course of human history, and their work had been guided by a deep sense of faith.

One of the most striking aspects of Andalusian scholarship was its openness to different cultures and traditions. The scholars of Andalusia had not only preserved the knowledge of the ancient Greeks and Romans but had also expanded upon it, incorporating ideas from other civilizations and making new discoveries of their own. This spirit of intellectual curiosity and collaboration had been a defining feature of Andalusian society, and it was something that Idris found deeply inspiring.

The scrolls mentioned several key figures who had played a central role in this intellectual flourishing. One of them was Ibn Rushd (Averroes), a philosopher who had written extensively on the relationship between religion and philosophy. Ibn Rushd had argued that reason and revelation were not in conflict but were complementary ways of arriving at the truth. His works had been translated into Latin and had influenced the development of European philosophy during the Middle Ages.

Another figure mentioned in the scrolls was Ibn al-Zahrawi (Abulcasis), a renowned surgeon whose medical texts had been used in both the Islamic world and Europe for centuries. Ibn al-Zahrawi's work on surgery and medical treatments had revolutionized the field of medicine, and his contributions had been guided by his belief that understanding the human body was a way of glorifying Allah's creation.

Idris found these stories of Andalusian scholars deeply inspiring. These were people who had dedicated their lives to the pursuit of knowledge, not for personal gain or recognition, but out of a sense of duty to their faith. They had understood that knowledge was a gift from Allah, and they had used it to benefit humanity and to draw closer to their Creator.

As Idris reflected on the legacy of Andalusian scholarship, he realized that the lessons of the past were still relevant today. In a world where knowledge was often pursued for material gain or prestige, the scholars of Andalusia offered a different perspective—one that valued knowledge as a form of worship and a means of fulfilling one's religious duties. Their work was a reminder that the pursuit of knowledge was not just about accumulating information but about seeking wisdom and understanding in order to serve a higher purpose.

Reflection: The Pursuit of Knowledge as a Path to Allah

AS IDRIS SAT BACK IN his chair, his mind buzzing with thoughts about the scholars of Andalusia and their approach to knowledge, he couldn't help but reflect on how their teachings applied to his own life. The idea that the pursuit of knowledge was a form of worship was a powerful one, and it had given Idris a new sense of purpose in his studies.

In today's world, knowledge was often seen as a means to an end—a way of advancing one's career, gaining wealth, or achieving status. But the scholars of Andalusia had viewed knowledge differently. For them, it was a way of drawing closer to Allah, of understanding His creation and fulfilling their religious duties. This was a perspective that Idris found deeply inspiring.

As he reflected on this, a verse from the Qur'an came to his mind:

"Say: Are those who know equal to those who do not know? Only they will remember [who are] people of understanding."

(Qur'an 39:9)

This verse emphasized the value of knowledge in the eyes of Allah. Those who sought knowledge were not only fulfilling their intellectual potential but were also engaging in an act of worship. By seeking to understand the world around them, they were honoring Allah's creation and drawing closer to Him.

Idris realized that this perspective had the power to transform the way he approached his studies. No longer would he see his university work as just a series of assignments to be completed or exams to be passed. Instead, he would approach his studies with a sense of purpose, knowing that the pursuit of knowledge was a way of fulfilling his religious duties and drawing closer to Allah.

This realization filled him with a sense of excitement and determination. He knew that the path ahead would not always be easy, but he was ready to face the challenges with a renewed sense of purpose. The lessons of the scholars of Andalusia had shown him that knowledge was not just a tool for personal advancement—it was a sacred endeavor, one that had the power to transform both the individual and the world.

As Idris closed the scrolls and prepared to continue his work the next day, he felt a deep sense of gratitude for the wisdom he had uncovered. The scholars of Andalusia had left behind a legacy that still had the power to inspire and guide future generations. Their pursuit of knowledge had been a form of worship, a way of connecting with Allah and fulfilling their purpose in this world.

Idris knew that he had a responsibility to carry forward that legacy, to seek knowledge with sincerity and humility, and to use what he learned to benefit others. The journey ahead would be long, but he was ready. With the light of the Qur'an and the wisdom of the scholars of Andalusia to guide him, Idris felt confident that he could navigate whatever challenges lay ahead.

Conclusion

In *Chapter 2: The Scholars of Andalusia – Seeking Knowledge*, the protagonist, Idris, begins to translate the scrolls he discovered in Andalusia, uncovering the profound wisdom of the scholars who lived during the Golden Age of Islam. These scholars valued knowledge as a form of worship, bridging the gap between science, philosophy, and faith. Through their writings, Idris learns that the pursuit of knowledge is not just an intellectual endeavor but a spiritual one—one that brings believers closer to Allah by deepening their understanding of His creation.

The reflection on the pursuit of knowledge as a form of worship reminds Idris that learning is not just about accumulating facts or achieving worldly success. It is about seeking wisdom and understanding as a way of honoring Allah and fulfilling one's purpose in life. The chapter highlights the importance of knowledge in Islam and emphasizes that the pursuit of learning is a sacred act that has the power to transform both individuals and societies.

As Idris continues his journey of discovery, he is inspired by the legacy of the scholars of Andalusia and is determined to carry forward their commitment to seeking knowledge with sincerity and humility.

Chapter 3: Faith in Action – The Importance of Iman (Faith)

Idris leaned back in his chair, his fingers tracing the edges of the parchment scrolls. Over the past weeks, he had immersed himself in the writings of scholars and historians from Andalusia, each scroll shedding new light on the forgotten legacy of that golden age of Islamic civilization. Today's discovery, however, felt different. As he translated the ancient script, he felt something stir deep within him—a sense that what he was uncovering went beyond academic curiosity. This was personal. The scroll he was working on was not a treatise on science or philosophy but a collection of stories, stories about early Muslims who had lived in Andalusia and remained steadfast in their *iman* (faith) despite the overwhelming challenges they faced.

The ink, though faded with time, still carried the weight of their struggles, their triumphs, and their unwavering commitment to live according to the principles of Islam. It was a reminder to Idris that faith, *iman*, was not simply an intellectual acknowledgment of Allah's existence; it was an active, living force that guided one's decisions, actions, and interactions with others.

Idris had always thought of himself as someone with strong faith. He prayed regularly, fasted during Ramadan, and attended Friday prayers at the mosque. But as he read the stories of the early Muslims in Andalusia, he began to realize that *iman* was not just about following rituals—it was about embodying faith in every aspect of life. It was about making difficult choices, standing firm in the face of adversity, and holding fast to one's principles, even when the world around you seemed to be falling apart.

The scroll he held in his hands told the story of a small Muslim community in a village near Cordoba during the early days of Islamic rule in Andalusia. The Muslims there faced constant threats from external forces, political instability, and economic hardships. Yet, despite these challenges, they remained steadfast in their faith, building a community that was rooted in *iman* and guided by Islamic principles.

One of the passages in the scroll stood out to Idris:

"In the face of trials, the believer does not waver. Their faith is like the roots of a mighty tree, unseen but strong, holding firm in the storm. They know that true strength comes not from the world around them but from Allah, who is the Sustainer of all things."

These words resonated deeply with Idris. They reminded him that faith was not about living a life free from difficulty. On the contrary, it was in times of hardship that one's faith was truly tested and revealed. The Muslims in Andalusia had lived through times of great uncertainty and peril, yet their *iman* had remained unwavering. For them, faith was not a passive belief; it was an active, living force that shaped their choices, their interactions, and their relationships.

The Trials of Faith: Stories from Andalusia

AS IDRIS CONTINUED reading the scroll, he came across several stories of individual Muslims who had embodied this idea of "faith in action." Each story was a testament to the strength of their *iman*, showing how they had remained true to their faith in the face of overwhelming challenges.

The first story was about a man named Yusuf, a scholar from Cordoba, who lived during a period of political upheaval. The rulers of the time were increasingly influenced by foreign powers, and corruption was rampant within the government. Yusuf, known for his piety and commitment to justice, was offered a high-ranking position in the government. The position came with wealth, influence, and power, but it also required him to compromise his principles and turn a blind eye to the injustices being committed against the people of Andalusia.

Yusuf could have easily accepted the position and lived a life of comfort, but his *iman* would not allow it. He knew that accepting the position would mean betraying the trust of the people and abandoning the principles of justice that were central to his faith. And so, despite the pressure from his peers and the promise of material wealth, Yusuf declined the offer. He continued to live modestly, dedicating his life to teaching and serving the community, even as those around him grew rich and powerful.

One of the passages describing Yusuf's decision read:

"Yusuf knew that wealth and power were fleeting, but the approval of Allah was eternal. He chose to live by his principles, for he feared not the judgment of men but the judgment of the One who sees all things."

Idris paused after reading this. He couldn't help but think about the pressures he faced in his own life—pressures to conform, to follow the crowd, to prioritize material success over spiritual integrity. How many times had he compromised his values, even in small ways, just to fit in or avoid conflict? Yusuf's story reminded him that true faith required more than just going through the motions of religious practice. It required making difficult choices, standing up for what was right, and prioritizing Allah's approval over worldly gain.

The next story in the scroll was about a woman named Fatima, a healer who lived in a rural village on the outskirts of Cordoba. Fatima was known for her knowledge of medicinal herbs and her ability to heal the sick, and people from all over Andalusia would come to seek her help. But Fatima's work was not without risk. During a time of political instability, the village was raided by soldiers who accused her of practicing sorcery. They threatened to imprison her if she did not stop her work.

Fatima was terrified. She knew that if she continued to help people, she would be putting herself in danger. But she also knew that her work was a form of service to Allah, and that helping others was a fundamental part of her faith. After much prayer and reflection, Fatima decided to continue her work, despite the threats. She trusted that Allah would protect her, and that as long as she was serving Him, she had nothing to fear.

The scroll described her decision in this way:

"Fatima's faith was like a shield, protecting her from the fear of the world. She knew that her life was in the hands of Allah, and that no harm could come to her except by His will. And so she continued her work, trusting in His protection."

This story moved Idris deeply. It reminded him that faith was not just about belief—it was about trust. Fatima's *iman* had given her the strength to continue her work, even in the face of danger, because she trusted that Allah was in control. Idris reflected on how often he allowed fear to dictate his decisions, how often he hesitated to act on his beliefs because of the potential consequences. Fatima's story was a powerful reminder that true faith required not only belief but also trust in Allah's plan, even when the path ahead seemed uncertain.

The final story in the scroll was about a group of young Muslims in Granada who had been tasked with building a mosque in their village. They faced immense opposition from the local rulers, who did not want a mosque to be built and who threatened to destroy it if they continued. The young Muslims could have given up, but their faith would not allow it. They saw the building of the mosque as an act of worship, a way to establish a place of prayer and community for future generations.

Despite the threats, they persevered. They worked day and night, often in secret, to complete the mosque. And when it was finally finished, they stood together in prayer, knowing that they had fulfilled their duty to Allah, even if it came at great personal cost.

The scroll described their perseverance with these words:

"The young men knew that the path of faith was not always easy, but they also knew that the reward was greater than any hardship they could face. For them, building the mosque was an act of worship, a testament to their devotion to Allah, and a gift to future generations."

This story resonated with Idris. It reminded him that faith was not just about personal belief—it was about community, about working together to build something greater than oneself. The young Muslims in Granada had understood that their faith was not just for them; it was for the generations to come. Their perseverance in the face of adversity was a powerful reminder that faith required action, integrity, and a willingness to sacrifice for the greater good.

Faith as a Way of Life

AS IDRIS CONTINUED to reflect on the stories from the scroll, he began to realize that *iman* was not just about belief—it was about action. It was about living according to Islamic principles in every aspect of life, even when it was difficult or inconvenient. The Muslims of Andalusia had understood this deeply. For them, faith was not something that could be separated from the rest of their lives. It was woven into everything they did—their work, their relationships, their decisions.

One of the verses from the Qur'an that came to Idris's mind was from *Surah Al-Baqarah*:

"Do you think that you will enter Paradise while such [trial] has not yet come to you as came to those who passed on before you? They were touched by poverty and hardship and were shaken until [even their] messenger and those who believed with him said, 'When is the help of Allah?' Unquestionably, the help of Allah is near."

(Qur'an 2:214)

This verse reminded Idris that faith was not just about believing in Allah when things were easy. It was about holding on to that belief even when the world seemed to be falling apart. It was about trusting that Allah's help was always near, even when it felt like it was far away. The Muslims of Andalusia had faced incredible challenges, but their *iman* had remained strong because they understood that faith was not something passive. It required action, perseverance, and a commitment to living according to Islamic principles, no matter what the world threw at them.

Idris thought about his own life and the challenges he faced. They were not nearly as severe as the ones faced by Yusuf, Fatima, or the young Muslims in Granada, but they were still real. He faced pressures from society, from his peers, from the world around him to compromise his faith, to conform to a way of life that was more focused on material success than spiritual integrity. It was easy to say he had *iman* when things were going well, but what about when it was difficult? What about when holding on to his faith meant standing out, being different, or facing opposition?

The stories from the scroll reminded Idris that true *iman* was not just about belief—it was about living according to that belief, even when it was hard. It was about making choices that were rooted in faith, even when those choices came with personal cost. It was about trusting in Allah's plan, even when the path ahead seemed uncertain.

Reflection: Living Faith in a Modern World

IDRIS LEANED BACK IN his chair, his mind buzzing with thoughts about how to apply the lessons he had learned from the scrolls to his own life. The world he lived in was very different from the world of Andalusia, but the challenges were, in many ways, the same. He still faced pressures to conform, to prioritize material success over spiritual fulfillment, to compromise his values in order to fit in.

But the stories of the early Muslims in Andalusia had shown him that *iman* was not just a belief—it was a way of life. It required action, integrity, and perseverance. It required making difficult choices, standing up for what was right, and trusting in Allah's plan, even when the path ahead seemed unclear.

One of the verses from the Qur'an that Idris found particularly meaningful as he reflected on these ideas was from *Surah An-Nisa:*

"O you who have believed, be persistently standing firm in justice, witnesses for Allah, even if it be against yourselves or parents and relatives. Whether one is rich or poor, Allah is more worthy of both. So follow not [personal] inclination, lest you not be just."

(Qur'an 4:135)

This verse emphasized the importance of standing firm in one's faith and principles, even when it was difficult. It reminded Idris that living according to Islamic principles was not always easy, but it was always necessary. Whether it was in matters of justice, integrity, or personal choices, *iman* required him to act in accordance with his faith, even when the world around him was pulling him in a different direction.

The more Idris thought about it, the more he realized that living according to *iman* in a modern world meant being conscious of every decision he made. It meant asking himself, in every situation, whether his actions were aligned with the teachings of Islam. Was he being honest? Was he acting with integrity? Was he treating others with kindness and compassion? Was he standing up for what was right, even when it was difficult?

He realized that *iman* was not something he could compartmentalize. It wasn't just about his prayers, his fasting, or his time at the mosque. It was about every aspect of his life—how he interacted with his family, how he treated his friends, how he approached his work and studies. True faith required him to embody the principles of Islam in everything he did.

And while that was a tall order, the stories from the scrolls had shown him that it was possible. The Muslims of Andalusia had faced incredible challenges, yet they had remained steadfast in their faith. They had lived according to their principles, even when it was hard, because they knew that their ultimate reward was with Allah.

As Idris closed the scrolls for the day, he felt a renewed sense of purpose. He knew that living according to *iman* in the modern world would not always be easy, but it was the path he was committed to following. The early Muslims in Andalusia had left behind a powerful legacy—a legacy of faith in action, of living with integrity, perseverance, and trust in Allah's plan.

And now, it was up to him to carry that legacy forward.

Conclusion

In *Chapter 3: Faith in Action – The Importance of Iman (Faith)*, the protagonist, Idris, learns through the stories of early Muslims in Andalusia that faith, *iman*, is not simply a matter of belief—it is a way of life. These stories illustrate how the early Muslims remained steadfast in their faith despite the challenges they faced, embodying Islamic principles in their actions, decisions, and relationships.

The reflection on *iman* emphasizes that true faith manifests in the way a believer lives their life, requiring action, integrity, and perseverance. The chapter explores how *iman* is not something that can be compartmentalized but must be woven into every aspect of life, guiding how one interacts with others, makes decisions, and responds to challenges.

As Idris reflects on these lessons, he realizes that living according to *iman* in the modern world means making difficult choices, standing firm in one's principles, and trusting in Allah's plan. The chapter highlights the importance of faith in action, showing that *iman* is not just a belief but a way of life that requires constant effort, trust, and commitment.

Chapter 4: Unity in Diversity – Ummah and Brotherhood

Idris stared at the open scroll, his fingers tracing the faded lines of script with a sense of awe. This scroll was different from the others he had read so far. It wasn't a theological treatise or a philosophical discourse, but rather a collection of personal accounts—stories of everyday people from different faiths who had lived in Andalusia during the height of its Islamic rule. What stood out to Idris the most was the description of how Muslims, Christians, and Jews had coexisted harmoniously for centuries in this diverse society. These stories painted a vivid picture of a time when Andalusia had been a beacon of coexistence, tolerance, and mutual respect—a place where the *Ummah* thrived alongside people of other faiths.

The idea of unity had always intrigued Idris. Growing up in a globalized world, he had witnessed how easily divisions could arise among people due to race, nationality, religion, and social class. These divisions often led to misunderstandings, prejudice, and even violence. Yet here, in the ancient land of Andalusia, people had managed to live together in peace despite their differences. It was as if the Andalusian society had embraced diversity rather than viewing it as a threat.

Idris leaned back in his chair, reflecting on what the scroll was teaching him. It was easy to romanticize the past, to imagine that Andalusia had been some kind of utopia, but the stories in this scroll showed that it hadn't been perfect. There had been tensions, conflicts, and challenges. But what made Andalusia remarkable was the way those challenges had been addressed—through dialogue, respect, and a shared commitment to justice. This unity in diversity had been made possible because of the Islamic principles of *Ummah* (the global Muslim community), brotherhood, and respect for others.

The Qur'an emphasized these values time and again, and the Muslims of Andalusia had lived by them. But how, Idris wondered, could these teachings be applied in today's world, where divisions seemed to run so deep? Could the lessons of Andalusia offer guidance for fostering unity and respect in modern times?

With these questions in mind, Idris returned to the scroll, eager to learn more about how the Andalusian Muslims had navigated the complexities of living in a diverse society while maintaining their commitment to the principles of Islam.

The Ummah: A Global Brotherhood

THE SCROLL BEGAN WITH a reflection on the concept of *Ummah*, the global Muslim community. The writer, a scholar from the 10th century, described how the Muslims of Andalusia had understood the *Ummah* not just as a religious identity but as a form of social responsibility. For them, being part of the *Ummah* meant that they were part of a global brotherhood, united by their shared faith in Allah and their commitment to the teachings of the Qur'an and the Sunnah of the Prophet Muhammad (PBUH).

One of the verses from the Qur'an that the scholar quoted was from *Surah Al-Hujurat:*

"The believers are but brothers, so make settlement between your brothers. And fear Allah that you may receive mercy."

(Qur'an 49:10)

This verse emphasized the idea that all Muslims, regardless of their race, nationality, or social status, were part of one global family. It called on believers to resolve their differences and to work together for the common good. The scholar explained that this principle had been central to the way Muslims in Andalusia had approached their relationships with one another. They had seen themselves as part of a larger community, one that transcended geographical boundaries and personal interests.

Idris found this idea inspiring. The concept of *Ummah* was often spoken about in his own community, but it sometimes felt distant—an abstract notion rather than a lived reality. Yet here, in Andalusia, the Muslims had truly embraced this concept. They had built a society where the bonds of brotherhood were strong, where people supported one another not just in words but in actions.

The scroll continued by recounting a story of how the Muslims of Cordoba had come together during a time of famine. The city had been suffering from a severe drought, and food supplies were running dangerously low. In response, the Muslim community had organized a city-wide effort to ensure that no one went hungry. People who had extra food shared it with those who had none, and those who were wealthier provided financial assistance to those who were struggling. The entire effort had been guided by the principle of *Ummah* —the idea that the well-being of one person was connected to the well-being of the entire community.

Idris was struck by the generosity and selflessness displayed in the story. The Muslims of Andalusia had understood that their faith required them to care for one another, not just in times of ease but in times of hardship. They had recognized that the bonds of brotherhood extended beyond personal relationships to include the entire community. This was what it meant to be part of the *Ummah* —to see the needs of others as your own and to work together for the collective good.

As Idris reflected on this, he realized that the principle of *Ummah* was not just about solidarity within the Muslim community—it was about extending that same spirit of care and compassion to others, regardless of their faith. The Qur'an called on Muslims to be just, kind, and merciful to all people, and the Muslims of Andalusia had embodied this in their interactions with Christians, Jews, and others who lived in their society.

Unity in Diversity: The Coexistence of Muslims, Christians, and Jews

ONE OF THE MOST REMARKABLE aspects of Andalusia, according to the scroll, was the way in which Muslims, Christians, and Jews had lived together in relative harmony. The scroll described how the three religious communities had worked side by side, contributing to the flourishing of Andalusian society. They had engaged in dialogue, shared ideas, and collaborated on projects that benefited everyone. While there were certainly moments of tension and conflict, the overall spirit of the time had been one of coexistence and mutual respect.

Idris read a passage from the scroll that recounted a meeting between Muslim, Christian, and Jewish scholars in the court of a Muslim ruler. The ruler had invited scholars from different religious backgrounds to engage in a dialogue about philosophy, ethics, and theology. The purpose of the meeting was not to debate or convert but to share knowledge and learn from one another.

The passage read:

"In the court of the ruler, there was no distinction between the Muslim, the Christian, and the Jew, for all were seekers of knowledge. They sat together as brothers, each contributing their wisdom to the discussion, and each respecting the faith of the other. The ruler, in his wisdom, understood that the pursuit of knowledge was a form of worship, and that wisdom was a gift from Allah, regardless of the faith of the one who possessed it."

This account amazed Idris. The idea that Muslims, Christians, and Jews could come together in such a way seemed almost unimaginable in today's world, where religious and cultural divisions often led to conflict and misunderstanding. Yet here, in Andalusia, people of different faiths had not only coexisted but had collaborated and learned from one another. The Muslims had recognized that wisdom and knowledge were gifts from Allah, and that these gifts could be found in people of all faiths.

Idris was reminded of a verse from the Qur'an that spoke to this idea:

"O mankind, indeed We have created you from male and female and made you peoples and tribes that you may know one another. Indeed, the most noble of you in the sight of Allah is the most righteous of you. Indeed, Allah is Knowing and Acquainted."

(Qur'an 49:13)

This verse emphasized the diversity of humanity and the importance of understanding and respecting one another. It reminded Idris that Islam did not seek to erase differences but to encourage people to learn from them. The Muslims of Andalusia had understood this well. They had seen their Christian and Jewish neighbors not as enemies but as partners in building a just and harmonious society.

Idris thought about how this principle could be applied in today's world, where religious and cultural divisions often seemed insurmountable. Could the spirit of Andalusia be revived in modern times? Could people of different faiths and backgrounds come together in a spirit of mutual respect and cooperation, just as they had in Andalusia?

Brotherhood and Respect in Action: Stories from Andalusia

THE SCROLL CONTINUED with several stories that illustrated how the Muslims of Andalusia had put these principles of brotherhood and respect into action. One story that particularly stood out to Idris was about a Muslim merchant named Ibrahim who had developed a close friendship with a Christian carpenter named Miguel. Despite their different faiths, the two men had worked together on various business ventures and had developed a deep bond of trust and mutual respect.

One day, Ibrahim fell seriously ill, and his family feared that he would not survive. In his weakened state, he called for Miguel, asking him to come to his home. When Miguel arrived, Ibrahim handed him a large sum of money, along with a letter detailing how the funds should be used to care for his family in the event of his death.

Miguel, moved by his friend's trust, assured Ibrahim that he would do everything in his power to honor his wishes. He promised to protect Ibrahim's family and to ensure that his business would continue to provide for them. Thankfully, Ibrahim recovered, and the two men's friendship only grew stronger after the incident.

The scroll described their relationship as follows:

"Though Ibrahim and Miguel worshipped in different ways, they were brothers in their hearts. They saw one another not as Muslim and Christian, but as friends and partners in this life. Their bond was a reflection of the Qur'anic command to treat others with justice and kindness, regardless of their faith."

Idris found this story deeply moving. It was a reminder that brotherhood was not limited to those who shared one's religion. Islam called on believers to treat all people with respect, kindness, and fairness, regardless of their background. Ibrahim and Miguel's friendship was a testament to the power of these values in action.

Another story in the scroll told of a Muslim judge in Seville who had presided over a legal dispute between a Muslim and a Jewish merchant. The case was complex, and both men were adamant that they were in the right. The judge, known for his wisdom and fairness, listened carefully to both sides before making his ruling.

After careful consideration, the judge ruled in favor of the Jewish merchant, explaining that the evidence supported his claim. The Muslim merchant, though disappointed, accepted the ruling with grace, acknowledging that justice had been served.

The scroll described the judge's actions in this way:

"The judge did not favor one man over the other because of his faith. He ruled with justice, as commanded by the Qur'an, for justice is the foundation of all righteous action. In his ruling, the judge honored the principles of Islam, which call for fairness and equity in all dealings, regardless of a person's religion."

This story highlighted the importance of justice in Islam. The judge had not allowed his personal biases to influence his decision. Instead, he had ruled according to the evidence and the principles of fairness and justice that were central to his faith. Idris was reminded of a verse from the Qur'an that spoke to this:

"O you who have believed, be persistently standing firm in justice, witnesses for Allah, even if it be against yourselves or parents and relatives. Whether one is rich or poor, Allah is more worthy of both. So follow not [personal] inclination, lest you not be just."

(Qur'an 4:135)

This verse emphasized the importance of standing firm in justice, even when it was difficult. It reminded Idris that justice was a fundamental part of Islam, and that it applied to all people, regardless of their faith or background.

Reflection: Promoting Unity and Brotherhood in a Divided World

AS IDRIS CLOSED THE scroll and leaned back in his chair, he found himself reflecting on the lessons he had learned from the stories of Andalusia. The Muslims of that time had understood the importance of unity and brotherhood, not just within the Muslim community but with people of other faiths as well. They had built a society that was based on mutual respect, cooperation, and justice—principles that were deeply rooted in the teachings of the Qur'an.

Idris thought about the world he lived in today, a world that often seemed so divided by religion, race, nationality, and ideology. It was easy to feel discouraged by the constant stream of news about conflicts, prejudice, and hatred. Yet the stories of Andalusia offered a powerful reminder that it was possible for people of different faiths and backgrounds to live together in peace and harmony. It wasn't always easy, and there were certainly challenges, but the Muslims of Andalusia had shown that it was possible.

One of the verses from the Qur'an that Idris found particularly meaningful as he reflected on these ideas was from *Surah Al-Ma'idah:*

"O you who have believed, be persistently standing firm for Allah, witnesses in justice, and do not let the hatred of a people prevent you from being just. Be just; that is nearer to righteousness. And fear Allah; indeed, Allah is Acquainted with what you do."

(Qur'an 5:8)

This verse emphasized the importance of standing firm in justice, even when faced with hatred or prejudice. It reminded Idris that the teachings of Islam called on believers to rise above division and conflict and to work toward justice and unity for all people.

Idris realized that promoting unity and brotherhood in today's world required both a commitment to Islamic principles and a willingness to engage with others in a spirit of respect and understanding. The stories of Andalusia showed that unity in diversity was not just an ideal but a reality that could be achieved through dialogue, cooperation, and a shared commitment to justice.

As he thought about how to apply these lessons in his own life, Idris made a commitment to live according to the principles of *Ummah*, brotherhood, and respect for others. He would strive to treat all people with kindness and fairness, regardless of their faith or background. And he would work to promote unity in his community, knowing that the teachings of Islam called him to be a force for peace and justice in the world.

Conclusion

In *Chapter 4: Unity in Diversity – Ummah and Brotherhood*, the protagonist, Idris, learns through the scrolls about the harmonious coexistence of Muslims, Christians, and Jews during the height of Andalusia's Islamic rule. The chapter explores the Qur'anic principles of unity, respect for diversity, and the importance of the global Muslim community (*Ummah*). Through stories of cooperation, justice, and mutual respect, Idris comes to understand that Islam promotes unity not just within the Muslim community but with all people.

The reflection emphasizes that the teachings of brotherhood, justice, and respect for others are central to Islam and that these principles can be applied in today's diverse world. The chapter highlights the importance of standing firm in justice and working toward unity, even in the face of division and conflict. Through the lessons of Andalusia, Idris is inspired to live according to these principles, knowing that the path of unity and brotherhood is one that is deeply rooted in the teachings of the Qur'an.

Chapter 5: Balance in Life – The Middle Path (Wasatiyyah)

The sun filtered through the tall windows of Idris' study, casting soft shadows across the scrolls scattered on the table. Idris had been working tirelessly to translate and understand the ancient manuscripts from Andalusia, but today, one particular scroll caught his attention. The worn parchment bore a title that instantly resonated with him: *Al-Mizan* —The Balance.

Idris carefully unrolled the scroll, eager to dive into its teachings. This scroll spoke about the Andalusian approach to life, a philosophy that placed great emphasis on balance—balance between the material and spiritual, between intellectual pursuits and emotional fulfillment. It was about living according to the Qur'anic principle of *Wasatiyyah* —the "middle path," a concept that was mentioned in the Qur'an and embodied by the Prophet Muhammad (PBUH) in his life and teachings.

Idris had always been fascinated by the idea of balance in Islam. In a world that often seemed to push people toward extremes—whether in pursuit of wealth, power, or even religious zeal—the idea of moderation, or *Wasatiyyah*, felt like a much-needed antidote. As he read the scroll, he realized that the scholars of Andalusia had understood this principle deeply, and they had lived by it in both their personal and societal lives.

The scroll opened with a Qur'anic verse that set the tone for the entire discussion:

"And thus We have made you a just community (Ummah Wasatan) that you will be witnesses over the people and the Messenger will be a witness over you..."

(Qur'an 2:143)

This verse described the Muslim community as *Ummah Wasatan* —a balanced, just community. It highlighted the importance of moderation and fairness in all aspects of life, from worship to daily living. As Idris continued to read, he felt a growing sense of clarity about how this concept of the middle path could be applied to his own life and the challenges of the modern world.

The Concept of Wasatiyyah: A Balanced Approach to Life

THE SCROLL BEGAN BY exploring the concept of *Wasatiyyah*, emphasizing that the middle path in Islam was not about mediocrity or compromise, but about achieving harmony and equilibrium in every aspect of life. The scholars of Andalusia had understood that life was full of competing demands—between the material and the spiritual, between the intellect and the heart—and that a fulfilling existence required balancing these forces rather than leaning too heavily toward one or the other.

One passage in the scroll stood out to Idris:

"To live according to the middle path is to recognize that the material and the spiritual are not enemies, but companions on the journey toward fulfillment. The mind and the heart are not at odds, but work together to guide the believer toward truth. In balance, there is peace. In extremes, there is destruction."

This idea resonated deeply with Idris. He had often felt torn between different aspects of his life—his intellectual pursuits, his spiritual practice, his career, and his relationships. At times, it seemed impossible to give each aspect the attention it deserved. But the scroll was teaching him that these elements didn't need to be in conflict. Rather, they were parts of a whole, and the key to a fulfilling life was finding the balance between them.

The scholars of Andalusia had lived by this principle, integrating their intellectual and spiritual lives in a way that enriched both. They had been deeply committed to the pursuit of knowledge, but they had also recognized that knowledge without spiritual grounding could lead to arrogance and materialism. At the same time, they had been devoted to their faith, but they had understood that faith without intellectual inquiry could lead to stagnation and extremism.

Idris was reminded of a verse from the Qur'an that encapsulated this idea:

"It is He who created for you everything that is on the earth. Then He turned to the heaven and made them seven heavens, and He is Knowing of all things."

(Qur'an 2:29)

This verse reminded Idris that the material world was not something to be shunned or despised. It was a gift from Allah, created for the benefit of humanity. The challenge, however, was to engage with the material world in a way that did not lead to excess or neglect of the spiritual. This balance, Idris realized, was at the heart of the concept of *Wasatiyyah*.

The Balance Between the Material and the Spiritual

AS IDRIS CONTINUED reading the scroll, he came across several stories of individuals from Andalusia who had exemplified the balance between the material and spiritual aspects of life. One story, in particular, stood out to him—it was about a wealthy merchant named Zayd who had lived in Cordoba during the 10th century.

Zayd had been incredibly successful in business, amassing great wealth through his trade with other regions. However, despite his material success, Zayd had never lost sight of his spiritual responsibilities. He had used his wealth to support his community, building mosques, schools, and hospitals, and providing for the poor. Zayd understood that his wealth was a trust from Allah, and he believed that it was his duty to use it in ways that benefited others.

The scroll described Zayd's life with these words:

"Zayd knew that wealth in itself was neither good nor evil—it was how one used it that determined its value. He sought to live according to the middle path, enjoying the blessings that Allah had bestowed upon him while ensuring that those blessings were shared with others. In this, he found balance, and in balance, he found peace."

This story struck a chord with Idris. In the modern world, the pursuit of wealth and material success often dominated people's lives. The pressure to achieve, to accumulate, and to consume was relentless, and it was easy to lose sight of the bigger picture. Zayd's life offered a different perspective—one that acknowledged the value of wealth but placed it within the broader context of spiritual and moral responsibility.

Idris was reminded of a verse from the Qur'an that spoke to this balance:

"But seek, through that which Allah has given you, the home of the Hereafter; and [yet], do not forget your share of the world. And do good as Allah has done good to you. And desire not corruption in the land. Indeed, Allah does not like corrupters."

(Qur'an 28:77)

This verse emphasized the importance of balancing one's focus on the Hereafter with one's responsibilities in the material world. It called on believers to seek the blessings of both the worldly life and the afterlife, while avoiding the extremes of neglecting one for the other. Zayd had embodied this principle, using his material wealth to serve both his spiritual goals and the needs of his community.

Idris reflected on how this applied to his own life. He had often felt conflicted about his career ambitions and his desire to deepen his faith. He worried that pursuing success in the material world might lead him away from his spiritual path. But the story of Zayd showed him that it was possible to do both—to engage with the material world while remaining grounded in faith and using one's success to benefit others.

The Balance Between Intellectual and Emotional Fulfillment

THE SCROLL ALSO SPOKE about the balance between intellectual and emotional fulfillment, another aspect of *Wasatiyyah* that the Andalusian scholars had emphasized. They had understood that the pursuit of knowledge and the cultivation of the intellect were essential components of a fulfilling life, but they had also recognized the importance of emotional well-being, relationships, and community.

One passage in the scroll stood out to Idris:

"The mind and the heart are partners on the journey toward truth. The intellect seeks to understand the world, while the heart seeks to connect with it. Together,

they lead the believer toward a deeper understanding of both the creation and the Creator."

This idea resonated with Idris deeply. As a student of history and philosophy, he had always placed a high value on intellectual pursuits. He enjoyed reading, studying, and engaging in debates about theology, ethics, and history. But there were times when he felt disconnected from his emotional life—when his focus on intellectual growth came at the expense of his relationships or his inner sense of peace.

The scholars of Andalusia had understood that true fulfillment required a balance between the mind and the heart. They had pursued knowledge with passion and rigor, but they had also nurtured their emotional and spiritual lives through prayer, reflection, and community. They had recognized that the intellect alone could not provide the answers to life's deepest questions. It had to be balanced with emotional insight, empathy, and a connection to others.

Idris was reminded of a verse from the Qur'an that spoke to the relationship between the mind and the heart:

"Indeed, in the creation of the heavens and the earth and the alternation of the night and the day are signs for those of understanding—Who remember Allah while standing or sitting or [lying] on their sides and give thought to the creation of the heavens and the earth, [saying], 'Our Lord, You did not create this aimlessly; exalted are You [above such a thing]; then protect us from the punishment of the Fire.'"

(Qur'an 3:190-191)

This verse highlighted the importance of both intellectual reflection and spiritual remembrance. It called on believers to use their minds to reflect on the signs of Allah's creation, while also engaging their hearts in worship and remembrance of Him.

Idris realized that finding balance between the intellect and the heart was essential for his own well-being. He needed to make time for both intellectual pursuits and emotional fulfillment, recognizing that each aspect of his life enriched the other. By nurturing his relationships, his inner peace, and his connection to Allah, he could ensure that his intellectual growth was grounded in something deeper and more meaningful.

Avoiding Extremes: The Dangers of Materialism and Extremism

AS IDRIS CONTINUED reading, the scroll warned against the dangers of falling into extremes—whether in the pursuit of material wealth or in the practice of religious devotion. The scholars of Andalusia had understood that both materialism and extremism were forms of imbalance that could lead a person away from the middle path and, ultimately, away from Allah.

The scroll told the story of a man named Khalid who had been born into a wealthy family in Seville. From a young age, Khalid had been obsessed with accumulating wealth, believing that financial success was the key to happiness and fulfillment. He had devoted all his energy to his business ventures, neglecting his family, his community, and his spiritual responsibilities. Although he became one of the richest men in the city, Khalid found that his wealth brought him little peace or satisfaction. He had everything he could ever want, but he felt empty inside.

Eventually, Khalid came to realize that his pursuit of wealth had led him down the wrong path. He had focused so much on material success that he had lost sight of the things that truly mattered—his relationship with Allah, his family, and his community. In an effort to correct this imbalance, Khalid sold much of his wealth and devoted himself to serving others. He built schools and hospitals, provided for the poor, and spent more time with his family. Through this, Khalid found a sense of peace and fulfillment that his wealth had never been able to provide.

The scroll described Khalid's transformation in these words:

"Khalid learned that wealth without purpose is a burden, and that the pursuit of material gain at the expense of the soul leads only to emptiness. In seeking balance between the material and the spiritual, he found a path to true fulfillment."

This story served as a powerful reminder to Idris of the dangers of materialism. In today's world, the pressure to accumulate wealth and achieve material success was pervasive. But Khalid's story showed that wealth, when pursued without balance, could become a trap—one that led to a life of emptiness and dissatisfaction. Idris realized that he needed to be mindful of this in his own life, ensuring that his pursuit of success was grounded in a sense of purpose and spiritual responsibility.

The scroll also warned against the dangers of religious extremism. It told the story of a man named Umar who had been so consumed by his desire to achieve spiritual perfection that he had abandoned all other aspects of his life. Umar had isolated himself from his family and community, spending all his time in prayer and fasting, and neglecting his responsibilities to others. Although he believed that his extreme devotion would bring him closer to Allah, it ultimately led him down a path of isolation and despair.

The scroll described Umar's downfall in this way:

"Umar believed that devotion meant abandoning the world, but in doing so, he abandoned the very responsibilities that Allah had entrusted to him. He sought to please Allah through extremes, but in doing so, he lost sight of the balance that leads to true piety."

This story reminded Idris that extremism in religious practice could be just as dangerous as materialism. Islam called on believers to live a balanced life, one that involved both devotion to Allah and fulfillment of one's responsibilities in the world. By focusing solely on one aspect of life—whether material or spiritual—a person risked falling into imbalance and losing sight of the middle path.

Idris was reminded of a hadith of the Prophet Muhammad (PBUH), who warned against extremes in religion:

"Beware of extremism in religion, for it destroyed those who came before you."

(Sunan Ibn Majah)

This hadith highlighted the importance of moderation in religious practice. It reminded Idris that Islam was a religion of balance and that true devotion required a thoughtful and measured approach to both worship and daily life.

Reflection: Following the Middle Path in Modern Life

AS IDRIS CLOSED THE scroll, he leaned back in his chair, reflecting on the lessons he had learned about *Wasatiyyah* —the middle path. The scholars of Andalusia had understood that balance was essential to a fulfilling life, and they had embodied this principle in their own lives. They had found a way to integrate the material and spiritual, the intellectual and emotional, in a way that enriched both.

Idris thought about the challenges he faced in his own life—the pressures of work, relationships, and personal ambitions. It was easy to get caught up in the pursuit of success, to focus too much on one area of life at the expense of others. But the concept of *Wasatiyyah* offered a different way of living—one that emphasized balance, harmony, and moderation.

One of the verses from the Qur'an that came to Idris's mind as he reflected on these ideas was from *Surah Al-Isra*:

"And do not make your hand [as] chained to your neck or extend it completely and [thereby] become blamed and insolvent. Indeed, your Lord extends provision for whom He wills and restricts [it]. Indeed, He is ever, concerning His servants, Acquainted and Seeing."

(Qur'an 17:29-30)

This verse spoke to the importance of moderation in all things—whether in spending, worship, or daily life. It reminded Idris that the middle path was not about denying oneself the blessings of this world, but about engaging with those blessings in a way that was balanced, thoughtful, and in accordance with Allah's guidance.

Idris realized that following the middle path in modern life required mindfulness and intention. It meant being aware of the different aspects of life—material, spiritual, intellectual, and emotional—and making time for each. It meant avoiding the extremes of materialism and extremism, and seeking a balanced approach that honored both the dunya (worldly life) and the akhirah (the Hereafter).

As Idris made a mental note to incorporate these lessons into his daily life, he felt a sense of peace and clarity. The path ahead might be challenging, but with the guidance of the Qur'an and the example of the scholars of Andalusia, he knew that he could navigate it with balance and grace.

Conclusion

In *Chapter 5: Balance in Life – The Middle Path (Wasatiyyah)*, the protagonist, Idris, learns through the scrolls about the Andalusian approach to life, where balance between the material and spiritual, intellectual and emotional, was seen as the key to a fulfilling existence. The chapter explores the Qur'anic concept of *Wasatiyyah* —the middle path—and how it applies to modern-day struggles with materialism and extremism.

The reflection emphasizes that following the middle path in Islam is not about mediocrity or compromise but about achieving harmony and balance in all aspects of life. The chapter highlights the importance of avoiding extremes, whether in the pursuit of material wealth or religious devotion, and encourages a balanced approach that integrates both the dunya and the akhirah.

As Idris reflects on these lessons, he is inspired to follow the middle path in his own life, recognizing that balance is essential for both personal fulfillment and spiritual growth. The concept of *Wasatiyyah* offers a powerful framework for navigating the complexities of modern life, helping believers achieve peace, clarity, and a deeper connection to Allah.

Chapter 6: Patience and Perseverance – Sabr in Times of Trial

The air in the study was still, the soft hum of the ceiling fan barely registering in Idris' mind as he leaned over the latest scroll. For the past several weeks, his journey into the heart of Andalusian history had been an exploration of intellect, spirituality, and balance. Today, however, felt different. The scroll before him wasn't filled with tales of intellectual achievements or harmonious coexistence. Instead, it recounted a much harsher reality—stories of struggle, persecution, and loss. These were stories of Muslim communities in Andalusia during periods of political upheaval and social chaos, when life as they knew it had been turned upside down by foreign invasions, internal strife, and shifting alliances. Yet through all this turmoil, the thread of *Sabr* —patience and perseverance—ran strong.

Idris felt a deep sense of connection as he began reading. He had his own challenges, but these stories spoke of an unshakable resilience that transcended time. The concept of *Sabr* wasn't unfamiliar to him. Growing up, his parents had often reminded him of the importance of patience in the face of adversity. It was a principle embedded in the Qur'an and the teachings of the Prophet Muhammad (PBUH). But reading these firsthand accounts of hardship and resilience brought a new depth to the concept. It wasn't just about waiting or enduring; it was about actively maintaining faith and hope in the most difficult moments.

The scroll began with a verse from the Qur'an that set the tone for what was to come:

"O you who have believed, seek help through patience and prayer. Indeed, Allah is with the patient."

(Qur'an 2:153)

This verse captured the essence of *Sabr*. It was a reminder that patience wasn't a passive act but a conscious effort to seek strength from Allah while enduring trials. As Idris read on, he discovered stories of individuals and communities who had embodied this principle during some of the darkest periods of Andalusian history.

The Trials of the Muslims in Andalusia

THE FIRST STORY IDRIS encountered was about the siege of Granada in 1491, one of the most tumultuous periods in the history of Islamic rule in Andalusia. For centuries, the Muslim rulers of Andalusia had created a flourishing civilization, but by the late 15th century, their power had waned. Granada, the last stronghold of Muslim rule, was under siege by the Christian forces of Ferdinand and Isabella.

The scroll recounted the story of a man named Hassan, a scholar who had lived in Granada during the siege. Hassan's family had been prosperous, and they had enjoyed a life of intellectual and spiritual fulfillment. But as the Christian forces advanced, their lives were thrown into chaos. Food became scarce, homes were destroyed, and fear permeated the city. Many fled, but Hassan stayed behind, convinced that the city would eventually be saved. For months, he and his family endured the hardships of the siege, clinging to their faith and seeking solace in prayer.

One night, as the sounds of cannon fire echoed in the distance, Hassan gathered his family in their small, crumbling home. He spoke to them about the importance of *Sabr*—about trusting in Allah's plan, even when the outcome seemed uncertain.

The scroll described that moment with these words:

"Hassan knew that victory was not in the hands of men but in the hands of Allah. He told his children that patience was the key to enduring the trials they faced. 'Hold fast to your faith,' he said. 'For this world is a test, and we must remain steadfast in the face of hardship. Sabr is our shield against despair.'"

As Idris read this passage, he imagined Hassan's words echoing in the darkness of that besieged city. Hassan's patience wasn't rooted in passive waiting—it was an active decision to trust in Allah's wisdom and to maintain hope even in the direst of circumstances. He understood that *Sabr* was not just about enduring suffering but about using that suffering to draw closer to Allah.

Eventually, Granada fell, and Hassan's family, like so many others, was forced to flee. They lost their home, their wealth, and the life they had known, but they carried with them their faith and the lessons of *Sabr*. Despite everything they had endured, Hassan never wavered in his belief that Allah had a greater plan for them.

This story struck Idris deeply. He thought about the difficulties he had faced in his own life—challenges at school, conflicts with friends, moments of doubt in his faith. None of them compared to the suffering of those who had lived through the siege of Granada, but the lesson was the same. *Sabr* was not just about surviving hardship; it was about transforming that hardship into an opportunity for growth, for strengthening one's relationship with Allah.

The Role of Sabr in Shaping Character

AS IDRIS CONTINUED reading the scroll, he encountered another story, this one about a young woman named Layla who had lived in Seville during a time of great political unrest. Layla's family had been torn apart by the conflicts between rival Muslim factions and the encroaching Christian forces. Her father and brothers had been killed in battle, and Layla, along with her mother and younger sister, had been left to fend for themselves.

The scroll described Layla's journey with vivid detail, recounting the many hardships she faced as she struggled to protect her family and preserve their faith. Despite the overwhelming grief and fear that threatened to consume her, Layla refused to give in to despair. Instead, she turned to her faith for strength, dedicating herself to prayer and seeking guidance from the Qur'an.

One night, as Layla sat by the flickering light of a candle, she recited a verse from *Surah Al-Baqarah* that had brought her comfort during her darkest moments:

"And We will surely test you with something of fear and hunger and a loss of wealth and lives and fruits, but give good tidings to the patient—Who, when disaster strikes them, say, 'Indeed we belong to Allah, and indeed to Him we will return.'"

(Qur'an 2:155-156)

This verse became a mantra for Layla, a reminder that her suffering was part of Allah's greater plan, and that by remaining patient and steadfast, she was fulfilling her duty as a believer. The scroll described how Layla's patience shaped her character, transforming her from a young woman overwhelmed by grief into a pillar of strength for her family and community.

"Through her patience, Layla became a source of hope for others. Her faith did not waver, even as the world around her crumbled. She understood that true Sabr was not merely the absence of complaint, but the active cultivation of hope, trust, and resilience. It was through Sabr that she discovered her own strength."

This story resonated with Idris on a deeply personal level. He thought about the times when he had faced challenges that seemed insurmountable—when his parents had struggled with financial difficulties, or when he had felt lost and unsure of his future. In those moments, he had often felt powerless, as if there was nothing he could do but wait for the storm to pass. But Layla's story showed him that *Sabr* was not about waiting; it was about growing. It was about using hardship as a tool for building strength and character.

Idris reflected on how *Sabr* had shaped his own character over the years. He realized that the moments of greatest difficulty in his life had also been the moments when his faith had grown the most. Patience had taught him to let go of control, to trust in Allah's wisdom, and to find peace in the knowledge that everything happened according to Allah's plan.

The Prophet Muhammad (PBUH) as the Model of Sabr

THE SCROLL ALSO INCLUDED reflections on the life of the Prophet Muhammad (PBUH), who had exemplified *Sabr* in every aspect of his life. The Prophet had faced countless trials—persecution, the loss of loved ones, physical hardship, and betrayal. Yet through it all, he had remained patient, trusting in Allah's plan and maintaining his unwavering commitment to his mission.

Idris had always admired the Prophet's patience, but reading these stories of Andalusian Muslims who had drawn inspiration from the Prophet's example gave him a new appreciation for the depth of that patience. The scroll recounted several key moments from the Prophet's life when his *Sabr* had been tested.

One of these moments was during the early years of Islam, when the Prophet and his followers were subjected to relentless persecution by the Quraysh in Mecca. The Prophet's uncle and protector, Abu Talib, passed away during this period, followed shortly by the death of the Prophet's beloved wife, Khadijah. These losses, combined with the increasing hostility from the Quraysh, would have been enough to break anyone's spirit. Yet the Prophet remained patient, trusting in Allah's wisdom and continuing to preach the message of Islam.

The scroll quoted a hadith that captured the Prophet's perspective on patience during times of hardship:

"How wonderful is the affair of the believer, for his affairs are all good, and this is for no one except the believer. If something good happens to him, he is grateful, and that is good for him. If something harmful happens to him, he is patient, and that is good for him."

(Sahih Muslim)

This hadith encapsulated the essence of *Sabr*. It wasn't about avoiding hardship but about responding to hardship with patience, trust, and faith. The Prophet's life was a testament to this principle. Even in the face of unimaginable loss and suffering, he had remained steadfast, knowing that every trial was an opportunity for growth and purification.

The scroll also recounted the story of Ta'if, when the Prophet had traveled to the city to spread the message of Islam, only to be met with rejection and violence. The people of Ta'if not only refused to listen to him but also pelted him with stones, injuring him and forcing him to flee. Despite this humiliation, the Prophet did not seek revenge or curse the people of Ta'if. Instead, he made a du'a to Allah, asking for guidance and mercy for the people, hoping that one day they would accept the message of Islam.

Idris found this story particularly moving. It reminded him that *Sabr* wasn't just about enduring personal hardship—it was also about showing patience and forgiveness toward others, even when they caused you pain. The Prophet's response to the people of Ta'if was a powerful example of this kind of patience. Rather than letting anger or bitterness consume him, the Prophet had chosen to respond with compassion and hope, trusting that Allah would guide the people in His own time.

Idris reflected on how he could apply this lesson in his own life. There had been times when he had struggled to forgive those who had wronged him, holding on to anger and resentment long after the initial hurt had passed. But the Prophet's example reminded him that patience wasn't just about enduring hardship—it was also about letting go of the desire for revenge and trusting in Allah's justice.

The Spiritual Benefits of Sabr

AS IDRIS CONTINUED to read, he came across a passage in the scroll that discussed the spiritual benefits of *Sabr*. The scholars of Andalusia had understood that patience was not just a moral virtue—it was a means of drawing closer to Allah and deepening one's faith. Through *Sabr*, a believer could purify their soul, strengthen their relationship with Allah, and attain a higher level of spiritual awareness.

One of the spiritual benefits of *Sabr* mentioned in the scroll was the development of *Tawakkul* —trust in Allah. When a person practiced patience in the face of hardship, they were, in effect, placing their trust in Allah's wisdom and timing. This trust allowed them to let go of their attachment to specific outcomes and to find peace in the knowledge that Allah was in control.

The scroll quoted a verse from the Qur'an that highlighted the connection between patience and trust in Allah:

"And whoever fears Allah—He will make for him a way out and will provide for him from where he does not expect. And whoever relies upon Allah—then He is sufficient for him."

(Qur'an 65:2-3)

This verse reminded Idris that patience was an expression of *Tawakkul*. When a believer practiced *Sabr*, they were acknowledging that their understanding of the situation was limited and that Allah's wisdom was greater than their own. By trusting in Allah's plan, they could find peace even in the midst of uncertainty and hardship.

The scroll also discussed how *Sabr* helped to purify the heart. When a person endured hardship with patience, they were forced to confront their own weaknesses, fears, and attachments. Through this process, they could identify the areas of their life where they needed to grow and could develop the inner strength and resilience necessary to overcome future challenges.

The scholars of Andalusia had recognized that patience was a form of spiritual training. Just as physical endurance was developed through exercise and discipline, spiritual endurance was developed through *Sabr*. By facing trials with patience, a believer could strengthen their heart and soul, becoming more resilient in the face of future hardships.

Idris reflected on how *Sabr* had helped him grow spiritually over the years. There had been times in his life when he had faced challenges that seemed overwhelming—whether it was the loss of a loved one, financial difficulties, or personal doubts about his faith. But in each of these moments, he had turned to patience as a way of navigating the storm. And through that patience, he had found not only a deeper sense of peace but also a stronger connection to Allah.

Reflection: How Sabr Shapes Faith and Character

AS IDRIS CLOSED THE scroll and sat back in his chair, he felt a profound sense of clarity about the role of *Sabr* in shaping faith and character. The stories of the Muslims in Andalusia—people like Hassan, Layla, and the Prophet Muhammad (PBUH)—had shown him that patience was not just a passive act of waiting but an active, transformative process. It was a way of turning hardship into an opportunity for growth, of deepening one's faith in Allah, and of developing inner strength and resilience.

Idris thought about the trials he had faced in his own life, and how *Sabr* had helped him navigate those difficult moments. He realized that patience had not only helped him survive those challenges but had also shaped him into the person he was today. Through *Sabr*, he had learned to trust in Allah's plan, to let go of his attachment to specific outcomes, and to find peace in the midst of uncertainty.

One of the verses from the Qur'an that Idris found particularly meaningful as he reflected on these ideas was from *Surah Al-Anfal:*

"O you who have believed, persevere and endure and remain stationed and fear Allah that you may be successful."

(Qur'an 3:200)

This verse reminded Idris that patience was an essential component of success—not just in this life, but in the Hereafter. It called on believers to persevere in the face of hardship, to remain steadfast in their faith, and to trust that Allah's wisdom would ultimately lead them to success.

As Idris thought about how he could apply these lessons in his own life, he made a commitment to practice *Sabr* more intentionally. He knew that challenges were inevitable, but he also knew that patience would help him navigate those challenges with faith and resilience. By practicing *Sabr*, he could strengthen his connection to Allah, purify his heart, and develop the inner strength necessary to face whatever trials came his way.

Conclusion

In *Chapter 6: Patience and Perseverance – Sabr in Times of Trial,* the protagonist, Idris, learns through the scrolls about the importance of *Sabr* —patience and perseverance—in the face of hardship. The chapter explores how Muslims in Andalusia, during periods of political and social upheaval, embodied the concept of *Sabr*, turning their trials into opportunities for spiritual growth and resilience.

The reflection emphasizes that *Sabr* is not just a passive act of waiting but an active process of trusting in Allah's wisdom, letting go of attachment to specific outcomes, and using hardship as a tool for spiritual purification. The chapter highlights the role of *Sabr* in shaping one's character and faith, showing that patience helps believers navigate the trials of life with strength, hope, and trust in Allah's plan.

As Idris reflects on these lessons, he is inspired to practice *Sabr* more intentionally in his own life, recognizing that patience is not only a way of enduring hardship but also a path to spiritual growth, inner strength, and a deeper connection to Allah.

Chapter 7: Justice for All – The Qur'anic Call for Fairness

Idris sat at his desk, staring at the scrolls spread out before him. His journey through Andalusian history had revealed much about the intellectual and spiritual legacy of that golden age, but today's discovery felt particularly significant. The scroll he had unrolled spoke of something deeply fundamental, not just to Andalusian society but to the core of Islamic teachings: *Adl*, or justice. The emphasis on fairness, equality, and accountability was woven throughout the Qur'an, and in Andalusia, these principles had been the bedrock of governance, law, and daily life.

As Idris began to read, he reflected on how the concept of justice often felt elusive in the modern world. Stories of corruption, inequality, and discrimination dominated the news, making it seem as though justice was more of an ideal than a reality. Yet, here in the scrolls, the lives of people in Andalusia were painted with the colors of fairness and equity, driven by the teachings of the Qur'an and the example of the Prophet Muhammad (PBUH). How had they managed to create a society where justice was not only a goal but a lived reality? And how could the lessons from that time be applied to the modern world?

Idris leaned in closer, eager to learn more. The scroll opened with a verse from the Qur'an, one that he had heard many times but now took on new meaning:

"O you who have believed, be persistently standing firm in justice, witnesses for Allah, even if it be against yourselves or parents and relatives. Whether one is rich or poor, Allah is more worthy of both. So follow not [personal] inclination, lest you not be just. And if you distort [your testimony] or refuse [to give it], then indeed Allah is ever, with what you do, Acquainted."

(Qur'an 4:135)

This verse set the stage for the entire discussion. It called on believers to uphold justice, regardless of personal ties or biases. It emphasized that justice was not a matter of convenience or favoritism—it was a divine command that applied to all people, in all situations. Idris felt a growing sense of responsibility as he read the verse. Justice was not just something to be pursued in the courts or in government; it was something that every believer was called to uphold in their daily lives.

The Role of Justice in Andalusian Governance

THE SCROLL BEGAN BY describing the role of justice in Andalusian governance. During the height of Islamic rule in Andalusia, justice was not just an abstract concept; it was a guiding principle in every aspect of society. The Qur'an's call for fairness and equality had shaped the laws, policies, and judicial systems of the time, ensuring that justice was accessible to all, regardless of their social or religious background.

One of the passages in the scroll described the way in which the Andalusian rulers had implemented the principles of *Adl*. The rulers had established courts of justice that were open to both Muslims and non-Muslims, and judges were chosen based on their knowledge of the law and their reputation for fairness. The judicial system was designed to ensure that all individuals, regardless of their status, were treated equally under the law.

The scroll recounted a specific case in which a Christian merchant had filed a complaint against a Muslim nobleman. The merchant claimed that the nobleman had taken advantage of his position to seize the merchant's property. The case was brought before an Islamic court, where the judge carefully examined the evidence and heard testimony from both parties.

Despite the nobleman's high status, the judge ruled in favor of the Christian merchant, ordering the nobleman to return the property and pay compensation. The nobleman was shocked by the ruling, as he had expected his status and wealth to influence the outcome. However, the judge's decision was a clear demonstration of the principle of *Adl*. In the eyes of the law, both men were equal, and justice required that the truth be upheld, regardless of wealth or power.

The scroll described the judge's ruling with these words:

"The judge, guided by the teachings of the Qur'an, knew that justice could not be swayed by wealth or status. His decision was a testament to the principles of fairness and equality that were the foundation of Andalusian governance. For in Islam, justice is not a privilege for the powerful but a right for all."

This story struck Idris deeply. It reminded him that justice was not just about following the rules or enforcing the law—it was about ensuring that every person, regardless of their background or position, was treated with fairness and respect. The Qur'an's call for justice was a reminder that power and privilege should never be used to oppress others, and that true justice required courage, integrity, and an unwavering commitment to the truth.

Idris was reminded of another verse from the Qur'an that emphasized the importance of standing up for justice:

"O you who have believed, be persistently standing firm for Allah, witnesses in justice, and do not let the hatred of a people prevent you from being just. Be just; that is nearer to righteousness. And fear Allah; indeed, Allah is Acquainted with what you do."

(Qur'an 5:8)

This verse spoke to the importance of maintaining justice, even in the face of personal enmity or bias. It reminded Idris that justice was not just about following legal procedures—it was about upholding the moral principles that Allah had commanded, even when it was difficult or unpopular.

Justice and Equality in Daily Life

AS IDRIS CONTINUED reading, the scroll shifted from discussing the role of justice in governance to exploring how the principle of *Adl* was applied in daily life. The scroll described how the people of Andalusia, both rulers and common citizens, had strived to create a society where justice and equality were reflected in every interaction—whether in business, family life, or community relations.

One of the stories that stood out to Idris was about a woman named Amina, who had lived in Cordoba during the 11th century. Amina was a respected businesswoman who ran a successful textile shop in the city. Despite her wealth and status, Amina was known for her fairness in all her dealings. She treated her employees with respect, paying them fair wages and ensuring that they were treated with dignity. She also made sure that her prices were reasonable and that her customers, regardless of their background, were treated with honesty and fairness.

One day, a poor man came into Amina's shop, asking for a discount on a piece of fabric that he needed to make clothes for his family. The man explained that he could not afford to pay the full price, but that he would work to pay off the remaining balance over time. Amina, seeing the man's need, agreed to his request, offering him not only a discount but also a small loan to help him get by. She trusted that the man would repay her when he was able, but even if he couldn't, she believed that it was her duty to help those in need.

The scroll described Amina's actions with these words:

"Amina understood that justice was not just about following the law but about treating others with fairness, compassion, and respect. She knew that wealth was a trust from Allah and that it was her responsibility to use it in a way that upheld the principles of justice and equity. For in Islam, justice is not limited to the courtroom but is reflected in every action and every interaction."

This story reminded Idris that justice wasn't just something that happened in courts or legal settings—it was something that each person was responsible for upholding in their daily lives. Amina's actions were a testament to the idea that *Adl* was about more than just enforcing laws—it was about creating a society where fairness, compassion, and integrity were the guiding principles in every aspect of life.

Idris thought about how he could apply these lessons in his own life. He realized that justice wasn't just the responsibility of judges or rulers—it was the responsibility of every individual. Whether in his relationships with friends and family, his interactions at work, or his dealings with strangers, Idris knew that he was called to uphold the principles of fairness and respect that the Qur'an commanded.

The Qur'an's Call for Justice

AS IDRIS CONTINUED to reflect on the lessons from the scroll, he was reminded of several key verses from the Qur'an that emphasized the importance of justice in Islam. One verse, in particular, stood out to him:

"Indeed, Allah commands you to render trusts to whom they are due and when you judge between people to judge with justice. Excellent is that which Allah instructs you. Indeed, Allah is ever Hearing and Seeing."

(Qur'an 4:58)

This verse highlighted two essential principles of justice in Islam: the importance of fulfilling one's responsibilities and the need to judge fairly between people. It reminded Idris that justice was not just about following legal procedures—it was about ensuring that every individual was treated with fairness, dignity, and respect, regardless of their status or background.

The Qur'an also emphasized that justice was a fundamental part of faith. One could not claim to be a true believer if they did not uphold the principles of fairness and equity in their actions. The Prophet Muhammad (PBUH) had exemplified this in his life, always striving to treat others with kindness and justice, even when faced with difficult circumstances.

One of the hadiths that Idris found particularly meaningful was:

"The best of people are those who are most beneficial to others."

(Al-Mu'jam Al-Awsat)

This hadith reminded Idris that justice was not just about following rules or enforcing laws—it was about being a source of goodness and benefit to others. Whether in personal relationships, business dealings, or community interactions, a true believer was someone who actively worked to uplift others and create a more just and equitable society.

The scroll also included reflections on the Prophet Muhammad's (PBUH) role as a judge and leader. The Prophet had always upheld the principles of justice, even when it meant ruling against his own family or close companions. He had shown that justice required impartiality, integrity, and a commitment to the truth, regardless of personal ties or pressures.

One of the most famous stories from the Prophet's life that illustrated this principle was the case of a woman from the Makhzum tribe who had committed theft. The people of her tribe, who were powerful and influential, sought to have her punishment reduced or waived. They sent one of the Prophet's close companions to intercede on her behalf, but the Prophet refused, stating that justice must be applied equally to all, regardless of their status.

The Prophet is reported to have said:

"By Allah, if Fatimah, the daughter of Muhammad, were to steal, I would have her hand cut off."

(Sahih Bukhari)

This statement was a powerful reminder that justice in Islam was not subject to favoritism or personal bias. The law applied equally to all, and the Prophet's commitment to fairness and equality was a model for all believers to follow.

Justice as the Foundation of Societal Harmony

THE SCROLL ALSO DISCUSSED how justice was the foundation of societal harmony in Andalusia. The rulers of Andalusia had recognized that a just society was a stable society. By ensuring that all individuals, regardless of their background, were treated fairly and equally under the law, they had been able to create a society where people of different faiths and cultures could coexist peacefully.

One of the key aspects of Andalusian governance was the inclusion of non-Muslims in positions of power and influence. Christians and Jews were not only allowed to live and worship freely, but they were also able to serve in government, hold positions of authority, and contribute to the intellectual and cultural life of the region. This policy of inclusivity was based on the Qur'anic principle of justice, which commanded fairness and equality for all people, regardless of their faith.

The scroll recounted the story of a Jewish scholar named Samuel ibn Naghrillah, who had served as the vizier to the Muslim ruler of Granada during the 11th century. Despite being a Jew in a predominantly Muslim society, Samuel was respected for his knowledge, wisdom, and commitment to justice. He had played a key role in shaping the policies of the region, ensuring that both Muslims and non-Muslims were treated fairly under the law.

The scroll described Samuel's role with these words:

"Samuel ibn Naghrillah understood that justice was not limited to one's own people or faith. He believed that true justice required fairness and equality for all, and he worked tirelessly to ensure that the laws of Granada reflected these principles. His leadership was a testament to the power of justice in creating a harmonious and inclusive society."

This story reminded Idris that justice was not just about following the rules—it was about creating a society where all people, regardless of their background, could live with dignity and respect. The rulers of Andalusia had understood that a just society was a peaceful society, and they had worked to ensure that the principles of *Adl* were reflected in every aspect of governance.

Idris reflected on how this lesson applied to the modern world. In today's globalized society, where people of different cultures, religions, and backgrounds were increasingly interconnected, the need for justice and inclusivity was more important than ever. He realized that upholding the principles of *Adl* required not only fairness in personal interactions but also a commitment to creating systems and institutions that promoted equality and justice for all.

Reflection: Upholding Justice in Our Lives

AS IDRIS CLOSED THE scroll, he sat back in his chair, reflecting on the lessons he had learned about justice and its role in both personal and societal harmony. The concept of *Adl*, as outlined in the Qur'an and exemplified in the governance of Andalusia, was not just about legal procedures or punishment—it was about fairness, integrity, and the dignity of every human being.

Idris realized that justice was something that each believer was responsible for upholding in their own life. Whether in their relationships with family and friends, their interactions at work, or their involvement in the community, believers were called to treat others with fairness, respect, and compassion. Justice wasn't just about following the rules—it was about embodying the principles of equity and goodness in every action.

One of the verses from the Qur'an that Idris found particularly meaningful as he reflected on these ideas was from *Surah An-Nisa:*

"Indeed, Allah commands you to render trusts to whom they are due and when you judge between people to judge with justice. Excellent is that which Allah instructs you. Indeed, Allah is ever Hearing and Seeing."

(Qur'an 4:58)

This verse reminded Idris that justice was not only a command from Allah but also a trust that believers were entrusted with. It was a responsibility that extended beyond the courts and into every aspect of life.

As Idris thought about how he could apply these lessons in his own life, he made a commitment to practice *Adl* more intentionally. He knew that upholding justice required both courage and humility. It meant standing up for what was right, even when it was difficult or unpopular, and ensuring that all people, regardless of their background, were treated with fairness and respect.

Conclusion

In *Chapter 7: Justice for All – The Qur'anic Call for Fairness*, the protagonist, Idris, learns through the scrolls about the importance of *Adl* —justice—in Andalusian governance and daily life. The chapter explores how the Qur'an's call for fairness and equality was reflected in the legal systems, governance, and personal interactions of the time, creating a society where justice was the foundation of societal harmony.

The reflection emphasizes that justice is not just a legal principle but a moral and spiritual responsibility that every believer is called to uphold. The chapter highlights the importance of treating all individuals with fairness and respect, regardless of their background, and shows how justice is essential for creating a peaceful and inclusive society.

As Idris reflects on these lessons, he is inspired to practice *Adl* more intentionally in his own life, recognizing that justice is not only a command from Allah but also a trust that believers must uphold in every action and interaction. The Qur'anic call for justice offers a powerful framework for navigating the complexities of modern life, helping believers create a more just and equitable world for all.

Chapter 8: The Art of Gratitude – Shukr as a Way of Life

Idris sat at his desk, his eyes scanning the scroll he had unrolled before him. The room was filled with the golden glow of the late afternoon sun, and the quiet rustle of the parchment filled the air. This scroll, like many others he had encountered, spoke of an Andalusian society that seemed both ancient and timeless, a place where Islamic principles had shaped not only governance and scholarship but also the personal lives of its people. Today's scroll, however, focused on a concept that resonated with Idris on a deeply personal level—*Shukr*, the Islamic principle of gratitude.

Gratitude, Idris thought, was something that came easily to him in good times. When his family was healthy, when his studies went well, when life flowed smoothly, it was easy to thank Allah for His blessings. But what about the times of difficulty? How did one practice *Shukr* when life didn't go according to plan, or when hardship overshadowed ease? The scroll before him promised to answer these questions by offering insights into how the people of Andalusia had lived with gratitude not just as a reaction to abundance, but as a way of life—a constant state of being, woven into every action, word, and thought.

As Idris began to read, the scroll opened with a verse from the Qur'an, one that captured the essence of *Shukr:*

"And [remember] when your Lord proclaimed: 'If you are grateful, I will surely increase you [in favor]; but if you deny, indeed, My punishment is severe.'"

(Qur'an 14:7)

This verse set the tone for the rest of the scroll. It reminded Idris that gratitude was not just a feeling or an expression—it was a way of life, one that brought with it divine blessings. The Qur'an promised that those who were grateful would be rewarded with more, but this wasn't limited to material wealth or success. The "increase" referred to here was far deeper—an increase in spiritual awareness, contentment, and peace of heart. Gratitude, the scroll suggested, was the key to a life of fulfillment, even in times of difficulty.

Shukr in Andalusian Society: Gratitude as a Foundation

The scroll began by describing the role of *Shukr* in Andalusian society. During the height of Islamic rule in Andalusia, gratitude was not just a personal virtue but a communal practice. The people of Andalusia had understood that gratitude was more than simply saying "thank you" to Allah for His blessings—it was about living a life that reflected that gratitude in every action.

One of the passages in the scroll explained how the rulers of Andalusia had emphasized the importance of gratitude, especially in times of abundance and success. The wealth and prosperity of the region, which had come through trade, scholarship, and agriculture, were seen as blessings from Allah. But instead of becoming complacent or arrogant in their wealth, the rulers and people of Andalusia had made *Shukr* a central part of their lives. They understood that gratitude wasn't just about words; it was about how they used their wealth, knowledge, and influence to benefit others.

The scroll recounted the story of a ruler named Abdullah, who had governed a prosperous region in Andalusia during the 10th century. Under his leadership, the region had flourished, with new schools, hospitals, and mosques being built. Trade was thriving, and the people enjoyed a high standard of living. Despite this success, Abdullah never lost sight of the importance of gratitude. He understood that his position and wealth were not his own—they were gifts from Allah, entrusted to him for the benefit of others.

Every year, during the month of Ramadan, Abdullah would personally oversee the distribution of wealth to the poor and needy in his region. He would walk through the streets, ensuring that every family had enough to eat and that the most vulnerable were cared for. His actions were not motivated by pride or a desire for recognition, but by a deep sense of gratitude to Allah for the blessings he had received.

The scroll described Abdullah's actions with these words:

"Abdullah knew that true gratitude was not expressed in words alone, but in service to others. He understood that the blessings he had received were not for his benefit alone, but for the benefit of the entire community. Through his actions, he demonstrated that gratitude was a way of life, a constant reminder of the responsibility that came with Allah's blessings."

This story struck Idris deeply. It reminded him that *Shukr* wasn't just about being thankful in one's heart—it was about how one lived. Abdullah had shown that gratitude was an active process, one that involved using one's blessings to uplift others. It wasn't enough to simply acknowledge the gifts of Allah—those gifts had to be shared, multiplied, and used in service to others.

Idris thought about his own life. He had been blessed with a loving family, good health, and the opportunity to pursue his studies. But how often had he used those blessings to help others? Had he truly expressed his gratitude through his actions, or had he taken those blessings for granted, assuming they would always be there?

The scroll reminded Idris of another verse from the Qur'an that emphasized the importance of gratitude:

"Indeed, Allah is full of bounty to the people, but most of the people do not show gratitude."

(Qur'an 40:61)

This verse underscored the idea that many people failed to recognize the blessings they had been given, and even when they did, they often neglected to express their gratitude in meaningful ways. Idris realized that *Shukr* wasn't just about recognizing blessings—it was about living in a way that honored those blessings.

Gratitude in Times of Difficulty

AS IDRIS CONTINUED reading, the scroll shifted from discussing gratitude in times of abundance to exploring the role of *Shukr* in times of difficulty. This, Idris thought, was where the true test of gratitude lay. It was easy to be thankful when life was going well, but how could one express gratitude when faced with hardship or loss?

The scroll recounted the story of a man named Ibrahim, who had lived in Seville during a period of great political instability. Ibrahim had been a successful merchant, known for his generosity and kindness. But when civil war broke out in the region, he lost everything—his home, his wealth, and his business. Forced to flee the city with his family, Ibrahim found himself living in a small, makeshift shelter on the outskirts of a neighboring town.

Despite the hardship he faced, Ibrahim never lost his sense of gratitude. Every morning, as the sun rose over the horizon, he would kneel in prayer, thanking Allah for the gift of life, for the health of his family, and for the new day. He taught his children to do the same, reminding them that even in the midst of difficulty, there were always blessings to be found.

The scroll described Ibrahim's attitude toward hardship with these words:

"Ibrahim understood that gratitude was not dependent on one's circumstances. He knew that the blessings of Allah were not limited to wealth or success, but could be found in the simple gifts of life—health, family, faith. Through his gratitude, he found peace, even in the midst of hardship. For he knew that everything, both good and bad, came from Allah, and that in gratitude, there was always the promise of hope."

This story moved Idris deeply. It reminded him that *Shukr* was not just about being thankful when things were easy—it was about finding gratitude in every situation, even when life seemed overwhelming. Ibrahim had lost everything, but he had never lost his faith in Allah or his ability to see the blessings in his life. His gratitude had given him the strength to endure hardship, and it had brought him peace in the midst of chaos.

Idris thought about the times in his own life when he had faced difficulty. There had been moments when he had struggled with his studies, or when personal conflicts had made him feel isolated and frustrated. In those times, it had been easy to focus on what was wrong, to complain, and to lose sight of the blessings that were still present. But Ibrahim's story showed him that gratitude was not about ignoring hardship—it was about recognizing that even in the midst of difficulty, there were still gifts from Allah to be thankful for.

Idris was reminded of a verse from the Qur'an that spoke to this idea:

"And We will surely test you with something of fear and hunger and a loss of wealth and lives and fruits, but give good tidings to the patient—Who, when disaster strikes them, say, 'Indeed we belong to Allah, and indeed to Him we will return.'"

(Qur'an 2:155-156)

This verse emphasized the idea that hardship was a test from Allah, and that those who responded to hardship with patience and gratitude would be rewarded. It reminded Idris that gratitude was not just a reaction to good fortune—it was a way of approaching life, a way of seeing the world through the lens of faith and trust in Allah's plan.

Shukr as a Form of Worship

THE SCROLL ALSO EXPLORED how *Shukr* was a form of worship in itself. The people of Andalusia had understood that expressing gratitude to Allah was not just about saying "thank you" in prayer—it was about living a life that reflected that gratitude. Every act of kindness, every moment of service to others, was seen as an expression of gratitude to Allah for His blessings.

One passage in the scroll described how scholars in Andalusia had emphasized the connection between gratitude and worship. They taught that the highest form of *Shukr* was not just to thank Allah for His blessings, but to use those blessings in ways that pleased Him. Whether it was wealth, knowledge, or physical ability, every gift from Allah was an opportunity to worship Him through service to others.

The scroll recounted the story of a scholar named Fatima, who had dedicated her life to teaching young girls in her community. Fatima had been blessed with great knowledge, and she saw it as her duty to pass that knowledge on to others. Despite the challenges she faced as a woman in a male-dominated society, Fatima never wavered in her commitment to education. She believed that her knowledge was a gift from Allah, and that the best way to express her gratitude for that gift was to use it to benefit others.

The scroll described Fatima's philosophy with these words:

"Fatima knew that knowledge was not her own—it was a gift from Allah, entrusted to her for the benefit of others. She understood that true gratitude was not just a feeling in the heart, but an action that flowed from the soul. Through her teaching, she expressed her Shukr to Allah, knowing that in serving others, she was serving Him."

This story inspired Idris. It reminded him that gratitude wasn't just about recognizing blessings—it was about using those blessings in ways that honored Allah. Fatima had shown that gratitude could be expressed through service, through the sharing of knowledge, and through acts of kindness. Her life was a testament to the idea that *Shukr* was not a passive feeling but an active way of living.

Idris thought about how he could incorporate this lesson into his own life. He had been blessed with the opportunity to pursue his studies, to learn from great teachers, and to expand his knowledge. But how had he used that knowledge to benefit others? Had he seen his education as a personal achievement, or as a gift from Allah that came with the responsibility to serve?

The scroll reminded Idris of a verse from the Qur'an that emphasized the connection between gratitude and worship:

"So remember Me; I will remember you. And be grateful to Me and do not deny Me."

(Qur'an 2:152)

This verse underscored the idea that gratitude was a form of worship, a way of remembering Allah and acknowledging His presence in every aspect of life. It reminded Idris that every moment of gratitude was an opportunity to draw closer to Allah, to deepen his faith, and to live a life that reflected the blessings he had received.

The Transformative Power of Gratitude

AS IDRIS CONTINUED reading, the scroll explored the transformative power of *Shukr* —how practicing gratitude could change one's perspective on life and bring about a deeper sense of contentment and peace. The people of Andalusia had understood that gratitude was not just about appreciating what one had—it was about seeing the world through a lens of abundance, rather than scarcity.

One of the passages in the scroll described how gratitude had shaped the lives of people in Andalusia, even in times of difficulty. The scroll recounted the story of a farmer named Yusuf, who had lived through a severe drought that had devastated the crops in his region. Many farmers had lost their livelihoods, and Yusuf's family was struggling to make ends meet. Despite the hardship, Yusuf remained grateful. Every evening, he would gather his family for prayer, thanking Allah for the health of his children, the roof over their heads, and the food that they still had, however meager it might be.

The scroll described Yusuf's attitude with these words:

"Yusuf understood that gratitude was not about the abundance of material wealth, but about the abundance of faith. He knew that the blessings of Allah were not measured in crops or coins, but in the love of family, the strength of faith, and the peace of heart that came from trusting in Allah's plan. Through his gratitude, Yusuf found contentment, even in the midst of loss."

This story reminded Idris that gratitude was a powerful force—it had the ability to transform one's perspective on life. Yusuf had lost his crops, his livelihood, but he had not lost his faith. His gratitude had allowed him to see the blessings that still remained, and in doing so, he had found contentment.

Idris reflected on how gratitude could transform his own life. There had been times when he had focused on what he lacked—whether it was a missed opportunity, a personal failure, or a difficult situation. But the scroll showed him that *Shukr* was about shifting that focus, about seeing the world through a lens of abundance rather than scarcity. It was about recognizing that even in the midst of difficulty, there were always blessings to be found.

Idris was reminded of another verse from the Qur'an that spoke to the transformative power of gratitude:

"And if you are grateful, He will surely increase you [in favor]."

(Qur'an 14:7)

This verse reminded Idris that gratitude wasn't just a passive acknowledgment of blessings—it was a way of inviting more blessings into one's life. By practicing *Shukr*, a person could cultivate a sense of contentment and peace, knowing that Allah's mercy was infinite and that His blessings were always present, even in the smallest of things.

Reflection: How Gratitude Shapes Our Lives

AS IDRIS CLOSED THE scroll and leaned back in his chair, he felt a deep sense of peace. The lessons of *Shukr* that he had learned from the scroll were not just about saying "thank you" in times of ease—they were about living a life of gratitude, a life that reflected the blessings of Allah in every action, every word, and every thought.

Idris realized that gratitude was more than just a feeling—it was a way of being. It was about seeing the world through the lens of abundance, recognizing that every moment, every breath, was a gift from Allah. It was about using one's blessings to benefit others, about serving Allah through service to humanity. And it was about finding contentment, even in the midst of hardship, by trusting in Allah's wisdom and mercy.

One of the verses from the Qur'an that Idris found particularly meaningful as he reflected on these ideas was from *Surah Al-Baqarah*:

"And [remember] when your Lord proclaimed: 'If you are grateful, I will surely increase you [in favor]; but if you deny, indeed, My punishment is severe.'"

(Qur'an 14:7)

This verse reminded Idris that gratitude was not just a reaction to good fortune—it was a way of life, a path to contentment and peace. It was a way of inviting more blessings into one's life by recognizing the blessings that were already present.

As Idris thought about how he could apply these lessons in his own life, he made a commitment to practice *Shukr* more intentionally. He knew that gratitude wasn't just about saying "thank you"—it was about living in a way that honored the blessings of Allah, about using those blessings to uplift others, and about finding peace in the knowledge that everything came from Allah, both the good and the difficult.

Conclusion

In *Chapter 8: The Art of Gratitude – Shukr as a Way of Life*, the protagonist, Idris, learns through the scrolls about the importance of *Shukr* —gratitude—as a central principle in Andalusian society. The chapter explores how gratitude was not just a feeling or an expression but a way of life, reflected in every action, word, and thought. The people of Andalusia had understood that gratitude was the key to contentment, even in times of difficulty, and that true *Shukr* was expressed not just in words but in service to others.

The reflection emphasizes that practicing gratitude can transform one's perspective on life, helping believers see the world through a lens of abundance and trust in Allah's mercy. The chapter highlights the power of *Shukr* to bring contentment, peace, and a deeper connection to Allah, showing that gratitude is not just a reaction to good fortune but a way of living that invites more blessings into one's life.

As Idris reflects on these lessons, he is inspired to practice *Shukr* more intentionally in his own life, recognizing that gratitude is not only a key to contentment but also a way of honoring Allah's blessings and living a life of service to others. The Qur'anic call for gratitude offers a powerful framework for navigating the challenges of life, helping believers cultivate a deeper sense of peace, contentment, and trust in Allah's plan.

Chapter 9: The Power of Dua – A Lifeline to Allah

Idris sat at his desk, the ancient scroll unrolled before him, its delicate parchment marked with the stories of those who had come before him—scholars, thinkers, believers who had once walked the vibrant streets of Andalusia. Each scroll he had translated had unlocked new layers of understanding about the lives of these remarkable individuals, but today's scroll felt different. It was not filled with the intellectual triumphs of scholars or the historical accounts of rulers. Instead, it was deeply personal, a collection of stories about *Dua* —the personal supplications that Muslims make to Allah.

As Idris began to read, he was struck by how central *Dua* had been in the lives of the people of Andalusia. The scroll didn't just recount moments of ease and gratitude, but also moments of intense struggle, where the individuals had turned to Allah with their hearts full of desperation and hope. Through the power of *Dua*, they had found solace, strength, and sometimes even miraculous solutions to their problems. Idris knew that *Dua* was an essential part of his own faith, but reading these stories reminded him that *Dua* was more than just a ritual—it was a lifeline, a direct connection to Allah that had the power to transform both heart and circumstance.

The scroll opened with a verse from the Qur'an, one that Idris had heard many times but now carried a new weight:

"And when My servants ask you concerning Me, indeed I am near. I respond to the invocation of the supplicant when he calls upon Me. So let them respond to Me [by obedience] and believe in Me that they may be [rightly] guided."

(Qur'an 2:186)

This verse set the tone for the rest of the scroll. It was a reminder that Allah was always near, always listening, and always ready to respond to the sincere *Dua* of His servants. Idris felt a deep sense of comfort as he read the verse. No matter what challenges he faced in life, no matter how difficult or overwhelming his circumstances might seem, Allah was never far. The act of raising his hands in supplication and calling upon Allah was not a last resort but a powerful and immediate connection to the One who had control over all things.

Dua as a Lifeline in Times of Hardship

THE SCROLL BEGAN WITH the story of a scholar named Malik, who had lived during a period of political unrest in Cordoba. Malik was known for his deep knowledge of Islamic law and theology, but he was also known for his humility and his reliance on *Dua*. Despite his status as a respected scholar, Malik had faced many personal challenges throughout his life, including the loss of his family and the constant threat of political persecution. Through it all, Malik had turned to *Dua* as his source of strength and solace.

One particularly poignant moment in Malik's life occurred when he was falsely accused of plotting against the local government. Fearing for his life, he fled into the hills outside Cordoba, hiding in caves and living off the land. Isolated and in constant danger, Malik spent his days in prayer and supplication, asking Allah for protection and guidance. He knew that his fate was in Allah's hands, and though he was afraid, his *Dua* gave him the strength to endure.

The scroll described one of Malik's supplications with vivid detail:

"O Allah, You are my protector in this life and the next. I seek refuge in You from the plots of my enemies, and I ask for Your mercy to cover me in these dark times. O Allah, grant me patience and strength, and guide me to safety, for there is no refuge but with You."

This *Dua* had been Malik's constant companion during those long days of hiding. Despite the fear and uncertainty that surrounded him, Malik found peace in his supplications. He knew that whatever the outcome, Allah's wisdom was greater than his own, and that his trust in Allah's plan was the key to surviving this trial.

Eventually, Malik's innocence was proven, and he was able to return to Cordoba. But the experience had left a lasting impact on him. He had learned that *Dua* was not just a request for help—it was a powerful expression of his faith and trust in Allah. Through *Dua*, Malik had found not only protection but also a deeper connection to Allah, one that transcended the immediate challenges he faced.

Idris reflected on Malik's story, realizing that *Dua* was not just about asking for specific outcomes. It was about surrendering to Allah's will and finding peace in the knowledge that He was always near, always listening. Malik's *Dua* had not just brought him physical safety—it had strengthened his heart, giving him the resilience to face whatever trials came his way.

Idris was reminded of a verse from the Qur'an that spoke to this idea:

"Is He [not best] who responds to the desperate one when he calls upon Him and removes evil and makes you inheritors of the earth? Is there a deity with Allah? Little do you remember."

(Qur'an 27:62)

This verse emphasized the power of *Dua* in times of desperation. It reminded Idris that when he felt overwhelmed by life's challenges, *Dua* was his lifeline, his direct connection to the One who could remove all burdens and bring relief. No matter how dire the situation, Allah was always near, ready to respond to the sincere supplication of His servant.

Dua as an Act of Worship and Gratitude

As Idris continued reading, the scroll shifted from discussing *Dua* in times of hardship to exploring *Dua* as an act of worship and gratitude. The scholars of Andalusia had understood that *Dua* was not just for moments of desperation—it was a daily practice, a way of maintaining a close relationship with Allah and expressing gratitude for His countless blessings.

One of the passages in the scroll recounted the story of a woman named Zaynab, who had lived in Granada during a period of great prosperity. Zaynab was a teacher and a healer, known for her deep knowledge of herbal medicine and her unwavering faith. Despite her busy life, Zaynab made time every day for *Dua*, not because she was in need of anything, but because she saw *Dua* as a form of worship, a way of thanking Allah for His blessings and maintaining her connection to Him.

Zaynab would often gather her students at the end of the day, leading them in supplication and reminding them of the importance of gratitude. Her *Dua* was not filled with requests for specific things, but rather with praise and thanks for the gifts that Allah had already bestowed upon her.

The scroll described one of Zaynab's supplications in detail:

"O Allah, You are the Most Merciful, the Giver of life and sustenance. I thank You for the blessings of health, of knowledge, and of the opportunity to serve others in Your name. O Allah, guide me to use the gifts You have given me in ways that please You, and grant me the strength to remain steadfast in my worship."

Zaynab's approach to *Dua* was a powerful reminder that supplication was not just about asking for help—it was about deepening one's relationship with Allah. By turning to Allah in gratitude and praise, Zaynab was able to maintain a sense of peace and contentment, even during times of prosperity. Her *Dua* was a daily reminder that all blessings came from Allah, and that gratitude was a key part of worship.

This story reminded Idris that *Dua* was not just for times of need—it was an ongoing conversation with Allah, one that allowed him to express his love, gratitude, and devotion. Zaynab's *Dua* had not been filled with requests for more blessings, but with thanks for what she already had. This was a powerful lesson for Idris, who realized that he often turned to *Dua* only when he needed something, forgetting that supplication was also a way of expressing his gratitude for the countless blessings he had already received.

Idris was reminded of a verse from the Qur'an that emphasized the importance of gratitude in *Dua:*

"So remember Me; I will remember you. And be grateful to Me and do not deny Me."

(Qur'an 2:152)

This verse underscored the idea that *Dua* was not just about asking for help—it was about remembering Allah and expressing gratitude for His constant presence in one's life. By making *Dua* a regular part of his daily routine, Idris realized that he could cultivate a deeper sense of gratitude and maintain a stronger connection to Allah, even in times of ease.

The Role of Sincerity in Dua

THE SCROLL ALSO EMPHASIZED the importance of sincerity in *Dua*. The people of Andalusia had understood that *Dua* was not just about the words one spoke—it was about the sincerity of the heart. A *Dua* that was made with true sincerity, with complete trust in Allah, had the power to transform not only one's circumstances but also one's heart.

One of the stories that stood out to Idris was about a man named Yusuf, who had been a farmer in a small village outside Seville. Yusuf had always been a hard worker, but despite his efforts, his crops had failed year after year. His family was struggling, and Yusuf felt the weight of his responsibility to provide for them. In his frustration, he had stopped making *Dua*, believing that his prayers were not being heard.

One day, Yusuf met an old scholar who had come to the village to teach. The scholar noticed Yusuf's distress and asked him why he had stopped making *Dua*. Yusuf explained that he felt his prayers were useless, that no matter how much he prayed, his situation remained the same.

The scholar listened patiently and then said something that would change Yusuf's life:

"It is not the words of your Dua that matter, Yusuf. It is the state of your heart. When you make Dua, do you truly believe that Allah is listening? Do you trust in His wisdom, even if the answer is not what you expected? Make your Dua with sincerity, and leave the rest to Allah."

These words struck Yusuf deeply. He realized that his *Dua* had been more of a formality than a true expression of trust in Allah. He had been asking for specific outcomes, but he had not truly surrendered his heart to Allah's wisdom. That night, Yusuf knelt in prayer and made a *Dua* unlike any he had made before. Instead of asking for specific things, he simply asked Allah for guidance and strength, trusting that whatever came next was part of Allah's plan.

The scroll described Yusuf's *Dua* with these words:

"O Allah, I have placed my trust in You, for You are the Knower of all things. I ask not for specific outcomes, but for the strength to endure whatever trials You place before me. O Allah, grant me patience and wisdom, and guide me to that which is best for me and my family."

After that night, something shifted in Yusuf's heart. His circumstances didn't change immediately, but his attitude did. He no longer felt weighed down by his failures, and instead found peace in the knowledge that Allah was in control. Over time, his situation improved, and his crops began to flourish again. But what mattered most to Yusuf was not the change in his circumstances—it was the change in his heart. Through sincere *Dua*, he had found a deeper connection to Allah and a sense of peace that transcended the ups and downs of life.

This story reminded Idris that sincerity was the key to *Dua*. It wasn't about asking for specific things or trying to control the outcome—it was about placing one's trust in Allah and surrendering to His wisdom. Yusuf's story showed that *Dua* had the power to transform not only one's circumstances but also one's heart, as long as it was made with sincerity and trust.

Idris was reminded of a hadith of the Prophet Muhammad (PBUH) that spoke to this idea:

"Verily, your Lord is generous and shy. If His servant raises his hands to Him [in supplication], He becomes shy to return them empty."

(Tirmidhi)

This hadith emphasized the generosity of Allah and His willingness to respond to the sincere *Dua* of His servants. It reminded Idris that Allah was always near, always ready to respond, but that the key to *Dua* was sincerity and trust. When a believer made *Dua* with a sincere heart, Allah would never leave them empty-handed.

The Impact of Dua on the Soul

AS IDRIS CONTINUED reading, the scroll explored the impact of *Dua* on the soul. The people of Andalusia had understood that *Dua* was not just a request for help—it was a way of nourishing the soul and deepening one's relationship with Allah. Through *Dua*, the soul was purified, strengthened, and brought closer to its Creator.

One of the passages in the scroll described how scholars in Andalusia had emphasized the spiritual benefits of *Dua*. They taught that *Dua* was not just about changing one's external circumstances—it was about transforming the heart and soul. By turning to Allah in sincere supplication, a believer could cleanse their heart of arrogance, fear, and doubt, and replace those feelings with trust, humility, and peace.

The scroll recounted the story of a young man named Ahmad, who had struggled with feelings of doubt and uncertainty about his faith. Despite being raised in a religious household and attending the best schools, Ahmad had always felt a sense of distance from Allah. He prayed regularly, but his prayers felt empty, and he often found himself questioning his beliefs.

One day, Ahmad confided in an older scholar, telling him about his struggles with faith. The scholar listened patiently and then suggested that Ahmad focus on *Dua*. He explained that *Dua* was not just about asking for things—it was a way of opening the heart to Allah, of strengthening the bond between the soul and its Creator.

The scholar gave Ahmad a simple piece of advice:

"When you make Dua, do not focus on what you want from Allah. Instead, focus on your love for Him, your trust in Him, and your desire to be close to Him. Let your Dua be a conversation, a way of drawing near to the One who created you."

Ahmad took this advice to heart. That night, instead of asking for specific things, he made a *Dua* from the depths of his heart, expressing his love for Allah and his desire to strengthen his faith. Over time, Ahmad found that his *Dua* began to transform his heart. The doubts that had once plagued him began to fade, replaced by a deep sense of peace and trust in Allah.

The scroll described Ahmad's transformation with these words:

"Through Dua, Ahmad's heart was purified, and his soul was strengthened. He no longer saw Dua as a request for things, but as a way of nourishing his relationship with Allah. In his supplications, he found not just answers to his questions, but a deep and abiding peace that came from knowing that Allah was always near."

This story resonated deeply with Idris. It reminded him that *Dua* was not just about changing external circumstances—it was about transforming the heart and soul. Through *Dua*, a believer could cleanse their heart of fear, doubt, and arrogance, and replace those feelings with trust, humility, and peace. Ahmad's story showed that *Dua* was not just a request for help—it was a way of drawing near to Allah, of strengthening the bond between the soul and its Creator.

Idris was reminded of another verse from the Qur'an that spoke to this idea:

"And your Lord says, 'Call upon Me; I will respond to you.' Indeed, those who disdain My worship will enter Hell [in humiliation]."

(Qur'an 40:60)

This verse emphasized the importance of calling upon Allah and the promise that He would respond. It reminded Idris that *Dua* was not just a request—it was an act of worship, a way of nourishing the soul and deepening one's relationship with Allah.

Reflection: The Role of Dua in a Muslim's Life

AS IDRIS CLOSED THE scroll, he felt a profound sense of peace. The stories of Malik, Zaynab, Yusuf, and Ahmad had shown him that *Dua* was not just about asking for help—it was about transforming the heart and soul, deepening one's relationship with Allah, and finding peace in the knowledge that Allah was always near.

Idris realized that *Dua* was a lifeline, a direct connection to Allah that had the power to bring comfort, strength, and resolve in times of difficulty. Whether in moments of desperation or gratitude, *Dua* was a way of expressing trust in Allah's wisdom and mercy, of surrendering to His plan and finding peace in the knowledge that He was always listening.

One of the verses from the Qur'an that Idris found particularly meaningful as he reflected on these ideas was from *Surah Ghafir:*

"And your Lord says, 'Call upon Me; I will respond to you.' Indeed, those who disdain My worship will enter Hell [in humiliation]."

(Qur'an 40:60)

This verse reminded Idris that *Dua* was not just a request for help—it was an act of worship, a way of drawing near to Allah and expressing trust in His wisdom and mercy. It was a reminder that Allah was always near, always ready to respond to the sincere supplication of His servants.

As Idris thought about how he could apply these lessons in his own life, he made a commitment to make *Dua* a regular part of his daily routine. He knew that *Dua* was not just for times of need—it was a way of maintaining a close relationship with Allah, of expressing gratitude, and of nourishing his soul.

Conclusion

In *Chapter 9: The Power of Dua – A Lifeline to Allah*, the protagonist, Idris, learns through the scrolls about the importance of *Dua* —supplication—in the lives of Andalusian scholars and believers. The chapter explores how *Dua* was not just a request for help but a powerful way of strengthening one's relationship with Allah, finding peace in times of difficulty, and expressing gratitude for His blessings.

The reflection emphasizes that *Dua* is a lifeline for Muslims, a direct connection to Allah that has the power to transform both heart and circumstance. The chapter highlights the importance of sincerity in *Dua*, showing that when a believer makes *Dua* with a sincere heart, Allah will never leave them empty-handed.

As Idris reflects on these lessons, he is inspired to make *Dua* a regular part of his life, recognizing that supplication is not only a way of asking for help but also a way of drawing near to Allah, nourishing the soul, and finding peace in the knowledge that Allah is always near. The Qur'anic call to make *Dua* offers a powerful framework for navigating the challenges of life, helping believers cultivate a deeper sense of trust, peace, and connection to their Creator.

Chapter 10: Trusting Allah – Tawakkul in the Divine Plan

Idris sat at his desk, the familiar crackle of ancient parchment under his fingertips. The scrolls had been his constant companions for weeks now, revealing the secrets, wisdom, and reflections of the Andalusian scholars who had lived centuries before him. Each scroll he unrolled seemed to offer new insights, and today's scroll promised to be no different. As he unfurled the aged document, Idris was greeted with a topic that touched his own heart in profound ways: *Tawakkul* —trust in Allah.

In the busyness of modern life, where deadlines, pressures, and future uncertainties clouded his mind, the concept of *Tawakkul* —the complete trust in Allah's plan—felt both comforting and challenging. How did one truly relinquish control over their future, especially when life felt unpredictable? Idris had often heard of *Tawakkul,* but understanding it intellectually was one thing—embracing it in times of hardship and uncertainty was another.

As Idris began to read the scroll, he found himself drawn into the stories of Andalusian scholars who had faced tremendous uncertainties in their lives but had found peace in their unwavering trust in Allah's wisdom and plan. The scroll's opening verse set the tone for the entire chapter:

"And whoever relies upon Allah—then He is sufficient for him. Indeed, Allah will accomplish His purpose. Allah has already set for everything a [decreed] extent."

(Qur'an 65:3)

This verse captured the essence of *Tawakkul* —that trusting in Allah's plan meant believing that, regardless of how uncertain life seemed, Allah's wisdom and control were absolute. Idris knew that the trials of life often tested a believer's faith in this principle, but the promise was clear: those who placed their trust in Allah would find that He was enough for them, no matter the circumstances.

Tawakkul in Times of Uncertainty

THE SCROLL BEGAN WITH the story of a scholar named Hassan, who had lived during a time of political upheaval in Andalusia. Hassan had been a respected teacher and philosopher, known for his wisdom and deep understanding of Islamic theology. But despite his intellectual prowess, Hassan's life had been filled with moments of uncertainty and hardship, particularly when his family was caught in the midst of a civil war that tore through their city.

Hassan's entire life had been devoted to his faith and his community, but as the war intensified, he found himself losing control over the future of his family. Their safety, their home, and even their very lives were threatened. Hassan had always believed in *Tawakkul*, but now, faced with the very real possibility of losing everything, he found it difficult to maintain his trust in Allah's plan.

One night, as the sounds of battle echoed through the streets, Hassan sat with his wife and children in their small, candlelit home. His wife, sensing his unease, asked him what was troubling him. Hassan explained that, despite his best efforts, he could not stop worrying about the future. What would happen to their family? Would they be forced to flee? Would they survive the war? He felt as though the weight of the world was pressing down on him, and he didn't know how to let go of the anxiety that gripped him.

Hassan's wife, who was known for her quiet strength, reminded him of a verse from the Qur'an:

"Say, 'Never will we be struck except by what Allah has decreed for us; He is our protector.' And upon Allah let the believers rely."

(Qur'an 9:51)

This verse had a profound impact on Hassan. It reminded him that, no matter what happened, everything that occurred in their lives was part of Allah's decree. Worrying about the future would not change what had already been written for them, but trusting in Allah would bring them peace, knowing that whatever the outcome, it was part of His divine plan.

The scroll described Hassan's reflection on this verse with these words:

"Hassan realized that his anxiety stemmed from his desire to control the future, but he understood now that control belonged only to Allah. His role was not to dictate the outcome, but to trust that Allah's wisdom was greater than his own, and that whatever befell them was part of Allah's perfect plan. In this, Hassan found peace, knowing that surrendering to Allah's will was the key to true freedom from fear."

This story resonated deeply with Idris. He, too, often found himself grappling with the unknown. The uncertainty of his career, the expectations placed on him by his family, and the fear of failure all weighed heavily on him. Like Hassan, Idris knew that he needed to place his trust in Allah, but the practice of *Tawakkul* —truly letting go of the need to control the future—felt like a constant challenge.

Idris was reminded of another verse from the Qur'an that spoke to the importance of trusting in Allah's plan:

"And rely upon the Ever-Living who does not die, and exalt [Allah] with His praise. And sufficient is He to be, with the sins of His servants, Acquainted."

(Qur'an 25:58)

This verse emphasized that Allah's wisdom and control were infinite, and that placing one's trust in Him was not a sign of weakness but of strength. It was a reminder that *Tawakkul* was not about giving up—it was about acknowledging that Allah's knowledge and power were far greater than any human understanding.

Letting Go of Anxiety

AS IDRIS CONTINUED reading, the scroll shifted from Hassan's story to a reflection on the nature of anxiety and how *Tawakkul* helped believers release the burdens that came from worrying about the future. The scholars of Andalusia had understood that anxiety stemmed from the fear of the unknown—the desire to control outcomes that were beyond human control.

But *Tawakkul* offered a way to let go of that fear, by placing one's trust in Allah and accepting that whatever happened was part of His divine plan.

One of the passages in the scroll recounted the story of a merchant named Umar, who had lived in Seville during a time of economic uncertainty. Umar had been a successful trader for many years, but a series of bad investments had left him on the verge of financial ruin. He worried constantly about how he would support his family, whether his business would recover, and what the future held for him.

Umar had always been a man of faith, but the pressures of his situation made it difficult for him to practice *Tawakkul*. He found himself consumed by anxiety, unable to sleep, and constantly fearing the worst. One day, Umar sought the advice of a local scholar, hoping to find some relief from his worries.

The scholar listened carefully to Umar's concerns and then asked him a simple question:

"Do you believe that Allah is the Provider, the Sustainer, and the Controller of all things?"

Umar nodded, of course he believed that. But the scholar's next question caught him off guard:

"Then why do you fear for the future, when it is Allah who controls it? Do you not trust that He has already written what is best for you, even if it is not what you expect?"

These words hit Umar deeply. He realized that his anxiety was not about his financial situation—it was about his inability to trust in Allah's plan. The scholar reminded him of a verse from the Qur'an:

"Indeed, my protector is Allah, who has sent down the Book; and He is an ally to the righteous."

(Qur'an 7:196)

This verse reminded Umar that Allah was not only his protector but also the one who had control over all aspects of his life. By placing his trust in Allah, Umar could release his anxiety and find peace in the knowledge that whatever happened, it was part of Allah's greater plan.

The scroll described Umar's reflection on this realization with these words:

"Umar understood that his anxiety came not from his circumstances, but from his reluctance to place his full trust in Allah. By letting go of his need to control the future, he found a sense of peace that transcended his financial troubles. He knew that whatever the outcome, Allah's wisdom was greater than his own, and that trusting in that wisdom was the key to overcoming his fears."

Idris was moved by this story. He realized that, like Umar, much of his own anxiety came from his desire to control outcomes that were beyond his reach. He worried about his future, his career, and his relationships, but he had not fully embraced the idea that Allah was in control. The scroll reminded him that *Tawakkul* was not just about accepting what happened—it was about finding peace in the knowledge that Allah's plan was always for the best, even if it wasn't what he had envisioned.

Idris was reminded of a hadith of the Prophet Muhammad (PBUH) that spoke to this idea:

"If you were to rely upon Allah with the reliance He is due, you would be given provision like the birds: they go out hungry in the morning and return full in the evening."

(Tirmidhi)

This hadith emphasized the idea that *Tawakkul* was about trusting that Allah would provide, just as He provided for the birds and all of creation. It reminded Idris that *Tawakkul* was not passive—it was an active trust in Allah's ability to take care of His servants, even in the most uncertain of times.

Surrendering to Allah's Plan

AS IDRIS CONTINUED reading, the scroll explored the idea of surrender—how *Tawakkul* was not just about trusting in Allah, but about surrendering one's will to His divine plan. The scholars of Andalusia had taught that true *Tawakkul* required a complete surrender of one's desires and expectations, trusting that Allah's wisdom was greater than any human understanding.

One of the stories in the scroll recounted the life of a scholar named Layla, who had devoted her life to teaching and writing. Layla had always believed in the power of *Tawakkul*, but her faith was tested when she faced a series of personal and professional setbacks. Her health began to deteriorate, and she was forced to give up her work as a teacher. At the same time, several of her manuscripts were lost in a fire, wiping out years of research and writing.

Layla was devastated. She had spent her entire life working towards certain goals, and now it seemed as though everything she had worked for was slipping away. She couldn't understand why Allah would allow these things to happen, and she found herself questioning her faith in His plan.

One day, as she sat by the window of her small home, watching the world go by, Layla remembered a verse from the Qur'an that had always brought her comfort:

"But perhaps you hate a thing and it is good for you; and perhaps you love a thing and it is bad for you. And Allah knows, while you know not."

(Qur'an 2:216)

This verse reminded Layla that Allah's wisdom was far greater than her own. She realized that her disappointment stemmed from her attachment to a specific outcome, but Allah's plan was not limited to her expectations. Layla understood that *Tawakkul* required her to surrender not just her anxiety but also her desires, trusting that whatever Allah had written for her was better than anything she could have imagined.

The scroll described Layla's reflection on this verse with these words:

"Layla realized that her disappointment came not from Allah's plan, but from her own expectations. She understood now that true Tawakkul required her to let go of her attachment to specific outcomes and to surrender fully to Allah's wisdom. In this surrender, Layla found a peace that transcended her circumstances, knowing that Allah's plan was always for her ultimate good."

This story resonated deeply with Idris. He realized that *Tawakkul* was not just about trusting in Allah—it was about surrendering one's will to His plan. Layla had shown him that the key to peace was not in getting what one wanted, but in trusting that Allah's plan was always for the best, even when it didn't align with one's expectations.

Idris was reminded of another verse from the Qur'an that emphasized the importance of surrendering to Allah's will:

"And whoever fears Allah—He will make for him a way out and will provide for him from where he does not expect. And whoever relies upon Allah—then He is sufficient for him."

(Qur'an 65:2-3)

This verse reminded Idris that Allah's wisdom was greater than any human understanding, and that those who placed their trust in Him would always find that He was sufficient for them. It was a reminder that *Tawakkul* was not just about trusting in Allah's plan—it was about surrendering to it, knowing that whatever happened, it was for one's ultimate good.

The Peace of Tawakkul

AS IDRIS CONTINUED to read, the scroll delved deeper into the idea of peace—how *Tawakkul* brought a sense of tranquility and contentment that could not be found in worldly pursuits. The scholars of Andalusia had understood that true peace came not from controlling the future, but from trusting in Allah's control.

One of the passages in the scroll recounted the story of a farmer named Yasin, who had lived through several years of drought. Despite his best efforts, Yasin's crops had failed year after year, and his family was on the brink of starvation. Yasin had always been a man of faith, but the constant hardship had tested his resolve.

One evening, as Yasin sat with his family, watching the sun set over their barren fields, his youngest daughter asked him why Allah hadn't answered their prayers. Yasin smiled gently and replied:

"Allah always answers our prayers, my dear. Sometimes He answers with what we ask for, and sometimes He answers with something better, even if we don't understand it yet."

These words brought Yasin's family comfort, but they also reminded Yasin of something important—*Tawakkul* wasn't about getting what one wanted, but about trusting that whatever happened was part of Allah's plan. Yasin realized that, despite the hardship they faced, they had been blessed in countless ways. His family was still together, still healthy, and still had their faith.

The scroll described Yasin's reflection on this realization with these words:

*"Yasin understood that *Tawakkul* was not about waiting for Allah to remove the hardship—it was about finding peace in the midst of it. He realized that true peace came not from changing his circumstances, but from trusting that Allah's wisdom was greater than his own, and that whatever happened, it was part of Allah's plan for his ultimate good."*

This story reminded Idris that *Tawakkul* was not about escaping hardship—it was about finding peace in the midst of it. Yasin had shown him that the key to peace was not in changing one's circumstances, but in trusting that Allah's plan was always for the best, even when it was difficult to see.

Idris was reminded of another verse from the Qur'an that spoke to this idea:

"For indeed, with hardship [will be] ease. Indeed, with hardship [will be] ease."

(Qur'an 94:5-6)

This verse reminded Idris that hardship was always followed by ease, and that trusting in Allah's plan meant believing that even in the darkest moments, there was always light at the end of the tunnel.

Reflection: The Power of Tawakkul

AS IDRIS CLOSED THE scroll, he felt a deep sense of peace. The stories of Hassan, Umar, Layla, and Yasin had shown him that *Tawakkul* was not just about trusting in Allah's plan—it was about surrendering one's will to His wisdom, finding peace in the knowledge that whatever happened was part of His divine plan.

Idris realized that *Tawakkul* was the key to navigating life's uncertainties. By letting go of his need to control the future, he could find peace in the present, knowing that Allah was always in control. The scroll had reminded him that *Tawakkul* was not passive—it was an active trust in Allah's wisdom and mercy, a trust that brought peace in the face of life's challenges.

One of the verses from the Qur'an that Idris found particularly meaningful as he reflected on these ideas was from *Surah At-Talaq:*

"And whoever relies upon Allah—then He is sufficient for him. Indeed, Allah will accomplish His purpose. Allah has already set for everything a [decreed] extent."

(Qur'an 65:3)

This verse reminded Idris that *Tawakkul* was not just a concept—it was a way of life, a way of finding peace in the knowledge that Allah's wisdom was greater than any human understanding.

As Idris thought about how he could apply these lessons in his own life, he made a commitment to practice *Tawakkul* more intentionally. He knew that trusting in Allah's plan was the key to overcoming his fears, his anxieties, and his need to control the future. By surrendering to Allah's wisdom, he could find a sense of peace that transcended the uncertainties of life.

Conclusion

In *Chapter 10: Trusting Allah – Tawakkul in the Divine Plan*, the protagonist, Idris, learns through the scrolls about the importance of *Tawakkul* —trust in Allah—in navigating life's uncertainties. The chapter explores how *Tawakkul* is not just about trusting in Allah's plan, but about surrendering one's will to His wisdom, finding peace in the knowledge that whatever happens is part of His divine plan.

The reflection emphasizes that *Tawakkul* is the key to overcoming anxiety and fear, helping believers find peace in the face of life's challenges. The chapter highlights the importance of letting go of the need to control the future and trusting that Allah's wisdom is greater than any human understanding.

As Idris reflects on these lessons, he is inspired to practice *Tawakkul* more intentionally in his own life, recognizing that trusting in Allah's plan is the key to finding peace, contentment, and a deeper connection to Allah. The Qur'anic call to trust in Allah offers a powerful framework for navigating the uncertainties of life, helping believers cultivate a deeper sense of trust, peace, and surrender to their Creator's wisdom.

Chapter 11: The Significance of Salah – Connecting with the Divine

The scroll before Idris was unlike any other he had encountered. It was beautifully ornate, its edges gilded with gold, and the script seemed more delicate than usual. As Idris gently unrolled the scroll, he immediately recognized the central theme: *Salah*, or prayer, the pillar of Islamic faith and the most direct form of connection between a believer and Allah. In Andalusia, *Salah* had been more than a religious duty—it had been the cornerstone of daily life, shaping both the spiritual and temporal aspects of society. The scroll spoke of the transformative power of *Salah* and the role it played in deepening one's connection to the Divine.

Idris couldn't help but reflect on his own relationship with *Salah*. He had grown up performing the five daily prayers, but as life became busier, he found himself sometimes rushing through them or postponing them. Reading this scroll was a chance for him to re-examine the meaning of *Salah* and how it could help him reconnect with his faith on a deeper level.

The scroll opened with a verse from the Qur'an that set the tone for the rest of the chapter:

"Indeed, I am Allah. There is no deity except Me, so worship Me and establish prayer for My remembrance."

(Qur'an 20:14)

This verse reminded Idris of the fundamental purpose of *Salah* —to worship Allah and remember Him throughout the day. It was a call for mindfulness, a way to anchor oneself in the present moment while also acknowledging the eternal presence of Allah. As Idris continued to read, he felt a deep sense of peace wash over him. The scroll seemed to speak directly to his heart, inviting him to reflect on how *Salah* could transform his spiritual life and provide solace in an increasingly hectic world.

Salah as the Cornerstone of Andalusian Life

THE SCROLL BEGAN BY describing the role of *Salah* in Andalusian society. During the height of Islamic rule in Andalusia, the call to prayer, or *Adhan*, echoed through the streets five times a day, serving as a reminder of the centrality of faith in every aspect of life. The people of Andalusia had understood that *Salah* was not just a private act of worship—it was a communal event that brought people together, reinforcing the bonds of brotherhood and sisterhood in the Muslim community, or *Ummah*.

In every city, town, and village, mosques served as the heart of the community. The *Adhan* would call people away from their daily tasks, whether they were scholars, merchants, or laborers, and draw them toward the mosque for prayer. The mosques were not just places of worship—they were centers of learning, discussion, and community building. But at the core of everything was *Salah*, the act of standing before Allah, bowing, prostrating, and remembering one's place in the grand scheme of creation.

One passage in the scroll recounted the story of a carpenter named Nasser, who lived in Cordoba during the 11th century. Nasser was known for his skill in woodworking, and he spent long hours in his workshop, crafting intricate pieces of furniture for the city's elite. Despite his busy schedule, Nasser never missed a single prayer. No matter how engrossed he was in his work, the moment he heard the *Adhan*, he would put down his tools, perform *Wudu* (ablution), and make his way to the mosque.

The scroll described Nasser's dedication to *Salah* with these words:

"Nasser understood that his work, no matter how important, was secondary to his relationship with Allah. He knew that success in this world was fleeting, but the success of the Hereafter was eternal. By performing Salah on time, Nasser reaffirmed his commitment to Allah and strengthened his connection to the Divine, finding peace and contentment in the rhythm of prayer."

This story struck a chord with Idris. He admired Nasser's unwavering commitment to *Salah*, even in the midst of his demanding profession. It reminded Idris that *Salah* was not an interruption to his day—it was the very thing that gave meaning and structure to his life. Like Nasser, Idris realized that prayer was a way to pause, reflect, and realign his priorities, ensuring that his connection with Allah remained at the forefront of his mind.

Idris was reminded of another verse from the Qur'an that emphasized the importance of regular prayer:

"Indeed, prayer has been decreed upon the believers a decree of specified times."

(Qur'an 4:103)

This verse underscored the idea that *Salah* was not a matter of convenience—it was a divine command that required discipline and commitment. By establishing prayer at specified times throughout the day, a believer could cultivate a sense of mindfulness and spiritual discipline that transcended the distractions of daily life.

Salah as a Source of Spiritual Nourishment

AS IDRIS CONTINUED reading, the scroll delved deeper into the spiritual significance of *Salah*. The scholars of Andalusia had understood that prayer was not just a physical act—it was a means of nourishing the soul and drawing closer to Allah. Through *Salah*, a believer could purify their heart, seek forgiveness for their sins, and experience the peace that came from standing in the presence of the Divine.

One passage in the scroll recounted the story of a scholar named Zayd, who had dedicated his life to studying the Qur'an and Hadith. Despite his vast knowledge of Islamic law and theology, Zayd knew that true wisdom came not from intellectual pursuits alone, but from a deep connection with Allah through *Salah*. Every night, after completing the *Isha* prayer, Zayd would spend hours in *Qiyam al-Layl* (the night prayer), seeking closeness to Allah through supplication and reflection.

The scroll described Zayd's nightly prayers with vivid detail:

"In the stillness of the night, Zayd would stand in prayer, his heart full of love and longing for Allah. Each movement—standing, bowing, prostrating—was a

reminder of his submission to the One who had created him. Through Salah, Zayd found not only peace but also the strength to face the challenges of life, knowing that Allah was always near, always listening."

This story reminded Idris of the transformative power of *Salah*. Zayd's dedication to the night prayer was a testament to the fact that *Salah* was not just a ritual—it was an opportunity to experience a deep and personal connection with Allah. Through prayer, Zayd had found solace, strength, and a sense of purpose that guided him through every aspect of his life.

Idris was reminded of a verse from the Qur'an that spoke to the importance of seeking closeness to Allah through prayer:

"And seek help through patience and prayer, and indeed, it is difficult except for the humbly submissive [to Allah]."

(Qur'an 2:45)

This verse highlighted the idea that prayer was not just a physical act—it was a means of seeking help and guidance from Allah, especially in times of difficulty. For those who were truly humble and submissive to Allah, *Salah* was a source of strength and comfort, providing a sense of peace that could not be found in the distractions of the world.

Idris reflected on his own approach to *Salah*. He realized that, at times, he had treated prayer as a duty to be fulfilled rather than as an opportunity to connect with Allah. Zayd's story reminded him that *Salah* was not just about going through the motions—it was about experiencing a deep sense of humility and submission before the Creator. It was a way of emptying the heart of worldly concerns and filling it with the remembrance of Allah.

Salah as a Shield Against Temptation

AS IDRIS CONTINUED reading, the scroll explored another important aspect of *Salah* —its role as a shield against temptation and sin. The scholars of Andalusia had understood that regular prayer was not just a means of worship—it was also a way of protecting oneself from the distractions and temptations of the world. Through *Salah*, a believer could develop the discipline and mindfulness needed to resist sinful inclinations and remain on the straight path.

One passage in the scroll recounted the story of a young man named Tariq, who had struggled with the temptations of wealth and power. Tariq had come from a wealthy family, and as a young man, he had been given control over his family's business. The sudden wealth and responsibility had overwhelmed him, and Tariq found himself drawn to the luxuries of life, neglecting his prayers and forgetting his spiritual obligations.

One day, Tariq's mentor, an older scholar named Ibrahim, confronted him about his neglect of *Salah*. Ibrahim reminded him of a verse from the Qur'an:

"Indeed, prayer prohibits immorality and wrongdoing, and the remembrance of Allah is greater. And Allah knows that which you do."

(Qur'an 29:45)

This verse struck Tariq deeply. He realized that his neglect of *Salah* had weakened his connection to Allah, leaving him vulnerable to the temptations of the world. Ibrahim encouraged him to return to his prayers, reminding him that *Salah* was not just a duty—it was a shield that would protect him from falling into sin.

The scroll described Tariq's journey of repentance and renewal with these words:

"Tariq understood now that Salah was not just an obligation—it was a lifeline, a way of grounding himself in the remembrance of Allah and protecting his heart from the distractions of the world. Through prayer, Tariq found the strength to resist the temptations of wealth and power, returning to the path of righteousness with a heart full of humility and gratitude."

This story resonated with Idris. He realized that, like Tariq, there had been times in his life when he had allowed the distractions of the world to pull him away from his spiritual obligations. He understood now that *Salah* was not just a way of worshiping Allah—it was a way of protecting himself from the temptations and challenges of life. By establishing regular prayer, Idris could strengthen his connection to Allah and develop the discipline needed to resist the distractions that threatened to pull him away from his faith.

Idris was reminded of a hadith of the Prophet Muhammad (PBUH) that spoke to the protective power of *Salah:*

"The first matter that the slave will be brought to account for on the Day of Judgment is the prayer. If it is sound, then the rest of his deeds will be sound. And if it is corrupt, then the rest of his deeds will be corrupt."

(Tirmidhi)

This hadith emphasized the central role of *Salah* in the life of a believer. It reminded Idris that prayer was not just one of many obligations—it was the foundation of his relationship with Allah. If his prayer was sound, it would serve as a shield, protecting him from the temptations and distractions of the world.

Salah as a Reminder of Purpose

AS IDRIS CONTINUED reading, the scroll explored the idea that *Salah* was a constant reminder of one's purpose in life. The scholars of Andalusia had understood that the rhythm of the five daily prayers served as a way to break up the day, providing moments of reflection and realignment with one's spiritual goals. Each time a believer stood in prayer, they were reminded of their ultimate purpose—to worship Allah and seek His pleasure.

One passage in the scroll recounted the story of a merchant named Khalid, who had built a successful trading business in Granada. Despite his success, Khalid had always made time for his prayers, knowing that his worldly achievements were meaningless without a strong connection to Allah. Every morning, before heading to the marketplace, Khalid would perform the *Fajr* prayer, setting his intention for the day and reminding himself that his work was ultimately a form of worship.

The scroll described Khalid's approach to life with these words:

"Khalid knew that his success in business was a blessing from Allah, but he also understood that it was a test. Through Salah, Khalid reminded himself that his true purpose in life was not to accumulate wealth, but to serve Allah and seek His pleasure. Each prayer was a moment of reflection, a way of realigning his heart with his spiritual goals and ensuring that his work was done with sincerity and gratitude."

This story reminded Idris that *Salah* was not just a way of worshiping Allah—it was a way of maintaining a sense of purpose and direction in life. Each prayer provided an opportunity to pause, reflect, and remember that everything he did, whether in his studies, his work, or his relationships, was ultimately for the sake of Allah.

Idris was reminded of a verse from the Qur'an that spoke to the purpose of creation:

"And I did not create the jinn and mankind except to worship Me."

(Qur'an 51:56)

This verse emphasized the idea that the ultimate purpose of life was to worship Allah. *Salah* was a way of fulfilling that purpose, providing structure to the day and reminding a believer that their time on earth was a test, a journey toward the Hereafter.

Reflection: The Transformative Power of Salah

AS IDRIS CLOSED THE scroll, he felt a renewed sense of appreciation for the significance of *Salah* in his life. The stories of Nasser, Zayd, Tariq, and Khalid had shown him that prayer was not just a ritual—it was a way of connecting with Allah, finding peace in the midst of a busy world, and protecting oneself from the distractions and temptations of life.

Idris realized that *Salah* was more than just an obligation—it was a gift, a way of grounding himself in the remembrance of Allah and ensuring that his heart remained focused on what truly mattered. Through regular prayer, he could find the strength, peace, and clarity needed to navigate the challenges of life.

One of the verses from the Qur'an that Idris found particularly meaningful as he reflected on these ideas was from *Surah Al-Baqarah:*

"O you who have believed, seek help through patience and prayer. Indeed, Allah is with the patient."

(Qur'an 2:153)

This verse reminded Idris that *Salah* was not just a physical act—it was a source of help and guidance from Allah. Through prayer, a believer could find the patience and strength needed to overcome life's difficulties and stay on the straight path.

As Idris thought about how he could apply these lessons in his own life, he made a commitment to approach *Salah* with greater mindfulness and sincerity. He knew that prayer was not just a duty to be fulfilled—it was a way of deepening his relationship with Allah and finding peace in the knowledge that Allah was always near, always listening.

Conclusion

In *Chapter 11: The Significance of Salah – Connecting with the Divine*, the protagonist, Idris, learns through the scrolls about the central role of *Salah* —prayer—in the lives of Andalusian scholars and believers. The chapter explores how *Salah* was not just a ritual obligation but a means of deepening one's relationship with Allah, finding peace in the midst of a busy world, and protecting oneself from temptation and sin.

The reflection emphasizes that regular prayer is vital for spiritual well-being, providing structure to the day and reminding believers of their ultimate purpose in life—to worship Allah and seek His pleasure. The chapter highlights the importance of approaching *Salah* with sincerity and mindfulness, recognizing that prayer is not just an act of worship but a source of strength, peace, and guidance in every aspect of life.

As Idris reflects on these lessons, he is inspired to make *Salah* a central part of his life, recognizing that prayer is the key to maintaining a strong connection with Allah and navigating the challenges of life with a heart full of gratitude, patience, and peace. The Qur'anic call to establish prayer offers a powerful framework for cultivating a deeper sense of purpose, mindfulness, and spiritual well-being in an increasingly distracted world.

Chapter 12: The Light of the Qur'an – A Guide for All Generations

———

The cool Andalusian breeze drifted through the open window of Idris's study as he unrolled the newest scroll. His fingers gently brushed over the ancient parchment, worn by centuries but still clear in its message. Today, the scroll's topic was one he held in deep reverence—the Qur'an, the timeless word of Allah, which had been a source of guidance and light for all believers, past and present. Idris had always turned to the Qur'an in times of need, but the stories within these Andalusian scrolls offered new perspectives on how deeply it had shaped the lives of scholars, rulers, and ordinary people alike.

The Qur'an was more than a book to be recited; it was a living guide, a source of wisdom that could help believers navigate the complexities of life, whether they lived in the bustling cities of 10th-century Andalusia or the fast-paced world of the modern era. The verses and principles within its pages remained unchanged, offering solutions to both the spiritual and worldly challenges that every generation faced.

Idris, like many others, had sometimes found it easy to overlook the Qur'an in the daily rush of life. But as he unfurled this particular scroll, he felt a profound sense of anticipation, knowing that the wisdom within these ancient Andalusian texts would help him re-center his life around the Qur'an's timeless message. He recalled a verse that encapsulated the essence of the Qur'an's purpose:

"This is the Book about which there is no doubt, a guidance for those conscious of Allah."

(Qur'an 2:2)

The Qur'an was not just a book of history or a collection of religious laws—it was a guiding light for every aspect of life. It was designed to be read, reflected upon, and internalized by those who were mindful of Allah's presence and sought His guidance. As Idris began to read, he understood that the Qur'an's message was meant for all generations, offering solutions to challenges that transcended time and place.

The Role of the Qur'an in Andalusian Life

THE SCROLL BEGAN BY describing the foundational role of the Qur'an in Andalusian society. During the height of Islamic rule in Andalusia, the Qur'an had been more than just a religious text—it had been the bedrock upon which the entire civilization was built. From the rulers in their palaces to the scholars in their libraries and the common people in the markets, the Qur'an was a constant presence, shaping both public policy and private morality.

The Qur'an was recited in mosques, studied in schools, and referenced in the legal and judicial systems. It informed the architecture of the cities, the ethics of trade, and the pursuit of knowledge. Every decision made by the rulers and scholars of Andalusia was rooted in the teachings of the Qur'an, ensuring that justice, fairness, and morality were at the forefront of every action.

One passage in the scroll recounted the story of a famous Andalusian ruler named Abdul Rahman III, who had led the Umayyad Caliphate in Córdoba to its greatest heights. Abdul Rahman III was known for his political acumen, military strength, and administrative reforms, but what set him apart from other rulers of his time was his deep connection to the Qur'an. He believed that the success of his empire was not due to his own intelligence or strength, but to the guidance he received from the Qur'an.

The scroll described how, every morning before conducting affairs of state, Abdul Rahman III would sit in his private study, reciting the Qur'an and reflecting on its meaning. His personal copy of the Qur'an was said to be worn from years of study, and he had memorized entire sections, which he often quoted during important meetings and speeches.

One of Abdul Rahman III's favorite verses was:

"And those who have believed and whose hearts are assured by the remembrance of Allah. Unquestionably, by the remembrance of Allah hearts are assured."

(Qur'an 13:28)

This verse had a profound effect on the way Abdul Rahman III governed his empire. It reminded him that no matter how powerful or successful he became, true peace and contentment could only be found through the remembrance of Allah and adherence to His guidance. The Qur'an was not just a religious text—it was the source of wisdom that guided his decisions and brought stability to his empire.

The scroll described Abdul Rahman III's reliance on the Qur'an with these words:

"Abdul Rahman III understood that the Qur'an was the key to both personal contentment and political success. He knew that a ruler's strength did not come from wealth, armies, or alliances, but from the guidance of Allah. By returning to the Qur'an each day, he ensured that his decisions were rooted in justice, mercy, and wisdom, securing both the prosperity of his people and the peace of his own heart."

This story struck a deep chord with Idris. Like Abdul Rahman III, he knew that the Qur'an held the answers to the challenges he faced in his own life, but how often had he turned to it for guidance? How often had he allowed the Qur'an to be the compass that directed his decisions? Abdul Rahman III's story reminded him that the Qur'an was not just a source of spiritual knowledge—it was a guide for all aspects of life, from the personal to the political.

Idris was reminded of another verse from the Qur'an that emphasized the role of the Qur'an as a guide:

"Indeed, this Qur'an guides to that which is most suitable and gives good tidings to the believers who do righteous deeds that they will have a great reward."

(Qur'an 17:9)

This verse underscored the idea that the Qur'an provided the best possible guidance for those who believed and sought to do good in the world. Whether one was a ruler or a common person, the Qur'an offered a path to righteousness and success, both in this life and the next.

The Qur'an as a Source of Wisdom for Scholars

AS IDRIS CONTINUED reading, the scroll shifted its focus to the scholars of Andalusia, who had dedicated their lives to studying the Qur'an and extracting its wisdom. These scholars were not just religious leaders—they were intellectual giants who sought to apply the Qur'an's teachings to all areas of knowledge, from philosophy and science to literature and art. The Qur'an was seen as the ultimate source of wisdom, and the scholars of Andalusia believed that by studying it deeply, they could unlock the secrets of both the physical and metaphysical worlds.

One passage in the scroll recounted the story of Ibn Rushd, a renowned Andalusian philosopher and jurist who had made significant contributions to both Islamic and Western thought. Ibn Rushd, also known as Averroes, had spent his life studying the Qur'an and applying its principles to his philosophical and scientific inquiries. He believed that there was no contradiction between reason and revelation, and that the Qur'an encouraged believers to seek knowledge and understand the world around them.

The scroll described how Ibn Rushd would often begin his philosophical discussions by quoting verses from the Qur'an, using them as the foundation for his arguments. One of his favorite verses was:

"Do they not contemplate the Qur'an? Had it been from [any] other than Allah, they would have found within it much contradiction."

(Qur'an 4:82)

This verse emphasized the idea that the Qur'an was a perfect, consistent source of knowledge, free from contradiction. For Ibn Rushd, this was proof that the Qur'an could be harmonized with reason and that its teachings were applicable to all fields of knowledge, from law to science.

The scroll described Ibn Rushd's approach to the Qur'an with these words:

"Ibn Rushd saw the Qur'an not only as a religious text but as a guide to intellectual and scientific inquiry. He believed that the Qur'an encouraged believers to seek knowledge, to question, and to reflect on the world around them. Through his study

of the Qur'an, Ibn Rushd found that reason and revelation were not opposing forces but complementary paths to understanding the truth."

This story inspired Idris to reflect on the intellectual richness of the Qur'an. He realized that the Qur'an was not just a book of spiritual guidance—it was a source of wisdom that could be applied to every aspect of life. Whether one was studying philosophy, science, or art, the Qur'an offered insights that could deepen one's understanding and provide a framework for exploring the world.

Idris was reminded of another verse from the Qur'an that encouraged reflection and contemplation:

"Indeed, in the creation of the heavens and the earth and the alternation of the night and the day are signs for those of understanding."

(Qur'an 3:190)

This verse emphasized the importance of reflecting on the world around us and recognizing the signs of Allah's presence in creation. For the scholars of Andalusia, the Qur'an was the key to unlocking these signs and understanding the deeper truths of the universe.

The Qur'an as a Guide for Personal Conduct

AS IDRIS CONTINUED reading, the scroll explored the role of the Qur'an in shaping personal conduct and morality. The scholars and rulers of Andalusia had understood that the Qur'an was not just a source of intellectual knowledge—it was a guide for how to live a righteous life, both in private and in public. Every verse of the Qur'an contained lessons on how to treat others, how to seek justice, and how to cultivate virtues such as patience, humility, and gratitude.

One passage in the scroll recounted the story of a young woman named Amina, who had lived in Seville during the 12th century. Amina had been known for her kindness and generosity, always going out of her way to help those in need. But what set her apart from others was her deep connection to the Qur'an. Amina had memorized large portions of the Qur'an, and she often recited its verses as she went about her daily tasks. For her, the Qur'an was not just a book to be studied—it was a guide for how to live her life.

The scroll described how Amina's favorite verse from the Qur'an was:

"And hasten to forgiveness from your Lord and a garden as wide as the heavens and earth, prepared for the righteous. Who spend [in the cause of Allah] during ease and hardship and who restrain anger and who pardon the people—and Allah loves the doers of good."

(Qur'an 3:133-134)

This verse had shaped Amina's entire approach to life. She believed that by following the Qur'an's teachings—by giving to others, controlling her anger, and forgiving those who wronged her—she could attain both peace in this life and the reward of Paradise in the Hereafter.

The scroll described Amina's life with these words:

"Amina lived by the Qur'an's teachings, not just in her words but in her actions. She understood that the Qur'an was a guide for personal conduct, teaching her how to be patient in the face of adversity, how to be generous in times of need, and how to forgive those who had wronged her. Through her connection to the Qur'an, Amina found peace, contentment, and a sense of purpose that guided her through every challenge she faced."

This story resonated deeply with Idris. He realized that the Qur'an was not just a book to be read or recited—it was a guide for how to live a life of righteousness, compassion, and justice. Amina's story reminded him that the Qur'an offered practical advice for every aspect of life, from how to treat others to how to cultivate a sense of inner peace.

Idris was reminded of another verse from the Qur'an that emphasized the importance of following the Qur'an's teachings:

"Indeed, this Qur'an guides to that which is most suitable and gives good tidings to the believers who do righteous deeds that they will have a great reward."

(Qur'an 17:9)

This verse reminded Idris that the Qur'an offered not only guidance but also good news for those who followed its teachings. By living according to the principles of the Qur'an, a believer could attain both success in this world and the reward of the Hereafter.

The Qur'an as a Timeless Source of Guidance

AS IDRIS CONTINUED reading, the scroll explored the idea that the Qur'an was a timeless source of guidance, offering wisdom that was relevant to every generation. The scholars and rulers of Andalusia had understood that the Qur'an's teachings were not limited to their time and place—they were universal, providing solutions to the challenges of every era.

One passage in the scroll recounted the story of a judge named Yusuf, who had lived during a time of great political unrest in Andalusia. Yusuf had been tasked with making difficult decisions that would affect the lives of thousands of people, and he often turned to the Qur'an for guidance. He believed that the Qur'an offered timeless principles of justice, fairness, and mercy that could be applied to even the most complex legal cases.

The scroll described how Yusuf would often begin his legal proceedings by reciting a verse from the Qur'an that spoke to the importance of justice:

"O you who have believed, be persistently standing firm in justice, witnesses for Allah, even if it be against yourselves or parents and relatives. Whether one is rich or poor, Allah is more worthy of both."

(Qur'an 4:135)

This verse reminded Yusuf that justice was a core principle of Islam and that he was obligated to uphold it, regardless of the social status or wealth of the people involved. The Qur'an provided a clear framework for making decisions that were fair, compassionate, and in accordance with Allah's will.

The scroll described Yusuf's approach to justice with these words:

"Yusuf understood that the Qur'an was not just a religious text—it was a guide for every aspect of life, including the administration of justice. He knew that by following the Qur'an's principles of fairness, mercy, and integrity, he could ensure that his decisions were not only just but also pleasing to Allah. The Qur'an was his constant companion, offering wisdom that transcended the complexities of his time."

This story reminded Idris that the Qur'an's teachings were not confined to the past—they were as relevant today as they had been during the time of the Prophet Muhammad (PBUH). The Qur'an's principles of justice, compassion, and morality were universal, offering solutions to the challenges of both the past and the present.

Idris was reminded of another verse from the Qur'an that emphasized the Qur'an's role as a guide for all generations:

"And We have certainly presented for the people in this Qur'an from every [kind of] example—that they might remember."

(Qur'an 39:27)

This verse reminded Idris that the Qur'an contained lessons for every situation, providing examples that were meant to guide believers in all aspects of life. Whether one was facing personal challenges or societal issues, the Qur'an offered timeless wisdom that could help navigate even the most difficult circumstances.

Reflection: The Qur'an as a Source of Light and Guidance

AS IDRIS CLOSED THE scroll, he felt a deep sense of gratitude for the Qur'an and the timeless wisdom it offered. The stories of Abdul Rahman III, Ibn Rushd, Amina, and Yusuf had shown him that the Qur'an was more than just a religious text—it was a guide for every aspect of life, offering solutions to both the spiritual and worldly challenges that believers faced.

Idris realized that the Qur'an was a source of light, illuminating the path to righteousness, justice, and inner peace. By returning to its teachings regularly, he could find the guidance he needed to navigate the complexities of modern life, just as the scholars and rulers of Andalusia had done centuries before.

One of the verses from the Qur'an that Idris found particularly meaningful as he reflected on these ideas was from *Surah Al-Isra:*

"Indeed, this Qur'an guides to that which is most suitable and gives good tidings to the believers who do righteous deeds that they will have a great reward."

(Qur'an 17:9)

This verse reminded Idris that the Qur'an was a guide to what was best and most suitable for all aspects of life. By following its teachings, he could find success, both in this world and the Hereafter.

As Idris thought about how he could apply these lessons in his own life, he made a commitment to return to the Qur'an more regularly, not just for recitation but for reflection and guidance. He knew that the Qur'an was the key to deepening his relationship with Allah, finding peace in times of difficulty, and living a life that was in harmony with Allah's will.

Conclusion

In *Chapter 12: The Light of the Qur'an – A Guide for All Generations*, the protagonist, Idris, learns through the scrolls about the central role of the Qur'an in the lives of Andalusian scholars, rulers, and ordinary people. The chapter explores how the Qur'an served as a guide for every aspect of life, offering solutions to both spiritual and worldly challenges.

The reflection emphasizes that the Qur'an is a timeless source of wisdom, providing light and guidance for all generations. The chapter highlights the importance of returning to the Qur'an regularly, not just for recitation but for reflection and practical application in everyday life.

As Idris reflects on these lessons, he is inspired to make the Qur'an a central part of his life, recognizing that its teachings offer solutions to the challenges of modern life, just as they did for the scholars and rulers of Andalusia. The Qur'anic call to seek guidance and light from its verses offers a powerful framework for navigating the complexities of the modern world while staying grounded in faith, righteousness, and the pursuit of Allah's pleasure.

Chapter 13: Mercy and Compassion – Rahmah as a Core Value

Idris sat in his study, the warm Andalusian sun streaming through the window, casting gentle shadows over the ancient scroll laid out before him. His heart felt lighter than it had in days, as if the wisdom of the past had opened new doors of understanding. This scroll was particularly captivating, focusing on the concept of *Rahmah* —mercy and compassion—as a fundamental value in Islam and the guiding principle behind the leadership and society that flourished in Andalusia.

As he began to read, Idris could feel the weight of centuries of wisdom passing through his fingers. The scholars of Andalusia had not just been intellectual giants; they had also understood the importance of *Rahmah* in building a society rooted in justice, kindness, and care for others. This concept of *Rahmah* was not only directed towards fellow Muslims, but extended to all of humanity, animals, and the environment. It was a reflection of Allah's own mercy, which encompassed all creation.

The scroll opened with a verse from the Qur'an that encapsulated the essence of *Rahmah*:

"And My Mercy encompasses all things."

(Qur'an 7:156)

This verse served as a reminder that Allah's mercy was infinite, extending to every living being and beyond. It set the tone for the entire scroll, emphasizing that *Rahmah* was not just an attribute of Allah but also a core value that believers were called to embody in their everyday lives.

As Idris read further, he was struck by the stories of merciful leadership and compassionate societies that had once thrived in Andalusia. The scroll painted a picture of a civilization where justice, fairness, and kindness were not just ideals but practices that shaped the lives of rulers, scholars, and ordinary citizens alike. The concept of *Rahmah* was at the heart of Andalusian society, fostering harmony, mutual respect, and a sense of responsibility toward others.

The Role of Rahmah in Leadership

THE SCROLL BEGAN BY describing the role of *Rahmah* in the leadership of Andalusia. During the golden age of Islamic rule in the region, rulers had been expected to embody mercy and compassion in their governance. This was not just a matter of policy—it was a reflection of their commitment to Islamic values. The Qur'an had laid out clear guidelines for leadership, emphasizing the importance of justice, mercy, and humility.

One passage in the scroll recounted the story of a famous Andalusian ruler, Al-Hakam II, who had been known for his merciful leadership and commitment to the welfare of his people. Al-Hakam II had inherited a prosperous kingdom, and under his rule, Cordoba became a center of learning, culture, and commerce. But what set him apart from other rulers was his deep sense of *Rahmah* toward his subjects.

The scroll described how Al-Hakam II would often walk through the streets of Cordoba in disguise, listening to the concerns of his people and ensuring that justice was being served. He believed that a ruler's strength lay not in their ability to wield power, but in their ability to show compassion and mercy to those under their care. One of his favorite verses from the Qur'an was:

"Indeed, Allah commands you to render trusts to whom they are due and when you judge between people to judge with justice. Excellent is that which Allah instructs you. Indeed, Allah is ever Hearing and Seeing."

(Qur'an 4:58)

This verse reminded Al-Hakam II that his position as a ruler was a trust from Allah, and that he would be held accountable for how he treated his people. His leadership was characterized by fairness, humility, and a deep sense of responsibility toward the most vulnerable members of society.

One of the most famous stories of Al-Hakam II's mercy involved a farmer who had been wrongfully accused of stealing from a nobleman's estate. The nobleman, using his influence, had managed to have the farmer imprisoned without a proper trial. When Al-Hakam II heard about the case, he personally intervened, ordering a thorough investigation. It was soon revealed that the farmer had been falsely accused, and the nobleman had fabricated evidence to protect his own reputation.

The scroll described the ruler's response with these words:

"Al-Hakam II did not simply free the farmer—he invited him to the palace, where he apologized for the injustice that had been done. The ruler then made a public proclamation, reminding all citizens that the law applied equally to the rich and the poor, and that mercy and justice were the foundation of a righteous society. In his leadership, Al-Hakam II demonstrated that Rahmah was not a sign of weakness, but a sign of true strength."

This story had a profound impact on Idris. He realized that *Rahmah* was not just about kindness in personal relationships—it was a guiding principle that extended to leadership, governance, and the administration of justice. Al-Hakam II's leadership had been defined by his commitment to fairness and his willingness to show mercy even to those who were powerless.

Idris was reminded of a hadith of the Prophet Muhammad (PBUH) that emphasized the importance of *Rahmah* in leadership:

"The merciful are shown mercy by the Merciful. Be merciful to those on the earth and the One above the heavens will have mercy upon you."

(Tirmidhi)

This hadith underscored the idea that showing mercy to others was a reflection of one's faith in Allah and a means of earning His mercy in return. Idris realized that *Rahmah* was not just a value to be practiced in personal relationships—it was essential for building a just and compassionate society.

Rahmah in Everyday Life

AS IDRIS CONTINUED reading, the scroll shifted its focus from leadership to the role of *Rahmah* in everyday life. The people of Andalusia had understood that mercy and compassion were not just values to be practiced by rulers—they were essential for building strong communities and fostering harmony among people of all backgrounds.

One passage in the scroll recounted the story of a marketplace in Granada, where Muslims, Christians, and Jews worked side by side in harmony. The marketplace had become a symbol of the peaceful coexistence that characterized Andalusian society, and it was largely due to the emphasis on *Rahmah* in the interactions between people of different faiths.

The scroll described how merchants in the marketplace were known for their honesty, fairness, and kindness toward one another. They believed that their business dealings were a reflection of their faith, and that showing mercy to others, regardless of their background, was a way of earning Allah's pleasure. One of the verses from the Qur'an that they often recited was:

"And speak to people good [words] and establish prayer and give zakah."

(Qur'an 2:83)

This verse emphasized the importance of speaking kindly to others and treating them with respect, regardless of their social or religious status. The merchants of Granada had internalized this message, and their marketplace became a model of harmony and cooperation.

One story that stood out to Idris was that of a Jewish merchant named Ezra, who had been struggling to make ends meet after his crops failed one season. Despite their own financial struggles, several Muslim merchants in the marketplace came together to support Ezra, offering him a loan without interest and helping him rebuild his business. When asked why they had done this, one of the merchants replied:

"Our Prophet taught us that we should love for our brother what we love for ourselves. Ezra is not just our neighbor—he is our brother in humanity. By showing him mercy, we hope that Allah will show mercy to us."

The scroll described the impact of this act of kindness with these words:

"Ezra was deeply moved by the generosity of his Muslim neighbors, and he often spoke of how their compassion had saved his family from ruin. The marketplace of Granada became known not just for its prosperity, but for the spirit of Rahmah that infused every transaction and interaction. Through their mercy, the merchants of Granada created a community that was bound together by love, respect, and mutual support."

This story resonated deeply with Idris. It reminded him that *Rahmah* was not just about grand gestures or acts of leadership—it was about the small, everyday interactions that could strengthen relationships and build a more harmonious community. The merchants of Granada had understood that mercy and compassion were not limited to their fellow Muslims—they extended to all of humanity.

Idris was reminded of another verse from the Qur'an that emphasized the importance of kindness and mercy in personal interactions:

"And lower to them the wing of humility out of mercy and say, 'My Lord, have mercy upon them as they brought me up [when I was] small.'"

(Qur'an 17:24)

This verse underscored the idea that mercy and compassion were foundational to all human relationships, whether between parents and children, neighbors, or members of different faith communities. By practicing *Rahmah*, believers could strengthen their bonds with one another and create a more peaceful and harmonious society.

Rahmah Toward Animals and the Environment

AS IDRIS CONTINUED reading, the scroll explored the concept of *Rahmah* in relation to animals and the environment. The scholars of Andalusia had understood that mercy was not limited to human beings—it extended to all of creation. The Qur'an had emphasized the importance of treating animals with kindness and caring for the natural world, and the people of Andalusia had taken these teachings to heart.

One passage in the scroll recounted the story of a shepherd named Yusuf, who had lived in a small village in the mountains of Andalusia. Yusuf was known for his deep love and care for the animals he tended, and he often spoke of how his work as a shepherd had taught him about the mercy of Allah.

The scroll described how Yusuf would often recite a verse from the Qur'an as he cared for his sheep:

"There is no creature on earth or bird that flies with its wings except [that they are] communities like you. We have not neglected in the Register a thing. Then unto their Lord they will be gathered."

(Qur'an 6:38)

This verse reminded Yusuf that animals were part of Allah's creation, and that they, too, were deserving of mercy and compassion. He believed that by treating his animals with kindness, he was fulfilling his duty as a steward of the earth and earning Allah's pleasure.

One of the most famous stories about Yusuf involved a time when one of his sheep had fallen into a ravine and broken its leg. Instead of leaving the animal behind, as many shepherds would have done, Yusuf carried the sheep on his back for miles until he reached a nearby village, where he was able to get help. When asked why he had gone to such great lengths to save a single sheep, Yusuf replied:

"If Allah shows mercy to all of His creation, how can I, a humble servant, do any less? This sheep is part of the trust that Allah has given me, and I will be held accountable for how I treat it."

The scroll described Yusuf's actions with these words:

"Yusuf's care for his animals was a reflection of his deep connection to the concept of Rahmah. He understood that mercy was not limited to human beings—it extended to all of creation. Through his work as a shepherd, Yusuf embodied the Qur'anic teachings of kindness, stewardship, and compassion for all living beings."

This story reminded Idris that *Rahmah* was not just about how one treated other people—it was about how one treated the world around them. The Qur'an had emphasized the importance of caring for animals and the environment, and the people of Andalusia had understood that mercy extended to every part of creation.

Idris was reminded of a hadith of the Prophet Muhammad (PBUH) that spoke to the importance of showing mercy to animals:

"Whoever is merciful even to a sparrow, Allah will be merciful to him on the Day of Judgment."

(Bukhari)

This hadith underscored the idea that *Rahmah* was not limited to human relationships—it was a value that encompassed all of creation. By showing kindness to animals and caring for the environment, believers could earn Allah's mercy and fulfill their role as stewards of the earth.

Reflection: The Power of Rahmah in Building Community

AS IDRIS CLOSED THE scroll, he felt a deep sense of peace and clarity. The stories of Al-Hakam II, the merchants of Granada, and Yusuf the shepherd had shown him that *Rahmah* was not just a lofty ideal—it was a value that could be practiced in every aspect of life, from leadership and governance to personal relationships and care for the environment.

Idris realized that *Rahmah* was the key to building strong, harmonious communities. By practicing mercy and compassion, believers could strengthen their relationships with one another, create a sense of mutual respect and support, and foster a society where justice and kindness were at the forefront of every interaction.

One of the verses from the Qur'an that Idris found particularly meaningful as he reflected on these ideas was from *Surah Al-Anbiya:*

"And We have not sent you, [O Muhammad], except as a mercy to the worlds."

(Qur'an 21:107)

This verse reminded Idris that the Prophet Muhammad (PBUH) had been sent as a mercy to all of creation, and that believers were called to follow his example by embodying mercy in their own lives. By practicing *Rahmah*, believers could bring peace, harmony, and justice to their communities and the world.

As Idris thought about how he could apply these lessons in his own life, he made a commitment to approach every interaction with mercy and compassion. He knew that *Rahmah* was not just a value to be practiced in times of ease—it was a value that required patience, humility, and a deep sense of responsibility toward others.

Conclusion

In *Chapter 13: Mercy and Compassion – Rahmah as a Core Value*, the protagonist, Idris, learns through the scrolls about the central role of *Rahmah* —mercy and compassion—in the lives of Andalusian rulers, scholars, and ordinary people. The chapter explores how *Rahmah* was not just a value to be practiced in leadership, but a core principle that shaped every aspect of society, from personal relationships to care for animals and the environment.

The reflection emphasizes that practicing *Rahmah* strengthens relationships, fosters mutual respect, and creates a more harmonious community. The chapter highlights the importance of embodying mercy and compassion in all interactions, recognizing that *Rahmah* is a reflection of Allah's infinite mercy and a means of earning His pleasure.

As Idris reflects on these lessons, he is inspired to make *Rahmah* a guiding principle in his own life, recognizing that by showing mercy to others, he can contribute to building a more just, compassionate, and harmonious world. The Qur'anic call to practice *Rahmah* offers a powerful framework for cultivating kindness, patience, and respect in every aspect of life, helping believers strengthen their relationships with one another and create communities rooted in justice and love.

Chapter 14: The Pursuit of Excellence – Ihsan in All Things

<hr>

Idris sat quietly in his study, the scroll he was about to open resting on the table before him. His mind buzzed with anticipation. Over the past weeks, the scrolls had opened up the world of Andalusia in ways he had never imagined. Each chapter had taught him profound lessons about faith, justice, mercy, and leadership. But today, the scroll he held promised to explore one of the most fundamental principles in Islam—the concept of *Ihsan*, or excellence. As Idris began to unroll the scroll, he found himself wondering what it truly meant to live a life of *Ihsan*, not only in worship but in every aspect of daily life.

The Qur'an mentions *Ihsan* numerous times, and the Prophet Muhammad (PBUH) had emphasized its importance in his teachings. The concept of *Ihsan* encompasses more than simply doing things well; it refers to a state of inner excellence where one's heart, mind, and actions are aligned in the pursuit of goodness, whether in religious devotion, personal conduct, or worldly endeavors. As Idris pondered the idea of *Ihsan*, he remembered the famous hadith where the Prophet Muhammad (PBUH) defined *Ihsan* as:

"To worship Allah as though you see Him, and if you cannot see Him, know that He sees you."

(Sahih Bukhari)

This hadith had always resonated with Idris, but it also challenged him. How could he reach a state of worship where he felt as though he was in the direct presence of Allah? And more importantly, how could he extend this sense of awareness and excellence beyond the mosque or prayer mat into his everyday life?

As Idris began to read the scroll, he was transported back in time to the golden age of Andalusia, where the pursuit of *Ihsan* was a way of life. The people of Andalusia had understood that striving for excellence was not limited to acts of worship—it extended to every aspect of life, from work and relationships to art, science, and personal growth. For them, *Ihsan* was a way of bringing the Divine into the mundane, transforming even the simplest tasks into acts of worship.

Ihsan in Worship

THE SCROLL OPENED WITH a verse from the Qur'an that encapsulated the essence of *Ihsan:*

"Indeed, Allah is with those who fear Him and those who are doers of excellence (Ihsan)."

(Qur'an 16:128)

This verse reminded Idris that *Ihsan* was not just about personal achievement—it was about striving for excellence in one's relationship with Allah. The people of Andalusia had understood that *Ihsan* began with worship, and that true excellence in worship came from sincerity, focus, and a deep sense of connection to the Creator.

One passage in the scroll recounted the story of a scholar named Abdul Malik, who had been known for his extraordinary devotion to Allah. Abdul Malik was not only a scholar of Islamic law and theology, but also a deeply spiritual man who spent much of his life in contemplation and prayer. His prayers were marked by a sense of humility and presence, as though he could feel the gaze of Allah upon him with every prostration.

The scroll described how Abdul Malik would often recite a verse from the Qur'an before beginning his prayers:

"Successful indeed are the believers, those who humble themselves in their prayers."

(Qur'an 23:1-2)

This verse was a reminder to Abdul Malik that the key to achieving *Ihsan* in worship was humility and mindfulness. He believed that prayer was not just a physical act—it was a means of drawing closer to Allah, of experiencing His presence in every moment. For Abdul Malik, each *rak'ah* (unit of prayer) was an opportunity to reflect on the greatness of Allah and to seek His mercy and guidance.

The scroll described Abdul Malik's approach to *Ihsan* in worship with these words:

"Abdul Malik knew that the true essence of prayer was not found in the outward movements, but in the inner state of the heart. He approached every prayer with a sense of awe, humility, and gratitude, as though he were standing before Allah Himself. Through his devotion, Abdul Malik achieved a state of Ihsan in his worship, transforming each prayer into a moment of deep spiritual connection."

This story deeply resonated with Idris. He realized that *Ihsan* in worship was about more than just completing the five daily prayers—it was about approaching each prayer with sincerity, humility, and mindfulness. Abdul Malik had shown him that true excellence in worship came from a heart that was fully present, focused on Allah, and filled with a sense of gratitude for His blessings.

Idris was reminded of another verse from the Qur'an that emphasized the importance of sincerity in worship:

"Say, 'Indeed, my prayer, my rites of sacrifice, my living and my dying are for Allah, Lord of the worlds.'"

(Qur'an 6:162)

This verse underscored the idea that worship was not just about ritual—it was about dedicating every aspect of one's life to Allah. For Idris, this meant approaching each prayer as an opportunity to renew his connection with Allah and to strive for *Ihsan* in both his inner and outer actions.

Ihsan in Daily Life

AS IDRIS CONTINUED reading, the scroll shifted its focus from worship to the broader concept of *Ihsan* in daily life. The people of Andalusia had understood that excellence was not limited to acts of worship—it extended to every aspect of life, from work and relationships to personal growth and self-discipline. For them, *Ihsan* was about striving to do everything with care, intention, and a sense of responsibility, recognizing that every action, no matter how small, was an opportunity to please Allah.

One passage in the scroll recounted the story of a craftsman named Yusuf, who had lived in the bustling city of Seville. Yusuf was a carpenter by trade, known for his meticulous attention to detail and his dedication to creating beautiful, functional pieces of furniture. But what set Yusuf apart from other craftsmen was his understanding that his work was not just a means of earning a living—it was a way of fulfilling his responsibility to Allah and to his community.

The scroll described how Yusuf would often recite a verse from the Qur'an as he worked:

"And whatever good you put forward for yourselves—you will find it with Allah. It is better and greater in reward."

(Qur'an 73:20)

This verse reminded Yusuf that every action, no matter how small, was an opportunity to earn Allah's pleasure. Whether he was building a simple chair or a grand table, Yusuf approached his work with *Ihsan*, striving to create something that was not only beautiful but also useful to others. For him, excellence in craftsmanship was a reflection of his devotion to Allah and his commitment to serving his community.

The scroll described Yusuf's approach to work with these words:

"Yusuf believed that excellence in his craft was a form of worship, a way of showing gratitude for the skills and talents that Allah had given him. He approached every project with care, patience, and attention to detail, knowing that his work was not only for his customers but also for Allah. Through his dedication, Yusuf achieved a state of Ihsan in his work, transforming his daily labor into an act of devotion."

This story inspired Idris to reflect on his own approach to work and personal responsibilities. He realized that *Ihsan* was not just about doing things well—it was about doing them with intention, care, and a sense of responsibility to

Allah and to others. Whether in his studies, his relationships, or his personal growth, Idris saw that every aspect of his life was an opportunity to strive for excellence and to bring himself closer to Allah.

Idris was reminded of a hadith of the Prophet Muhammad (PBUH) that emphasized the importance of *Ihsan* in all actions:

"Verily, Allah has prescribed excellence (Ihsan) in all things."

(Sahih Muslim)

This hadith underscored the idea that *Ihsan* was not limited to acts of worship—it was a principle that applied to every aspect of life. For Idris, this meant striving for excellence in everything he did, from his work to his interactions with others, recognizing that every action was an opportunity to please Allah.

Ihsan in Relationships

AS IDRIS CONTINUED reading, the scroll delved into the role of *Ihsan* in relationships. The people of Andalusia had understood that excellence was not just about personal achievements—it was about how they treated others, both within their families and in their broader communities. For them, *Ihsan* in relationships meant striving to be kind, compassionate, and fair, always seeking to improve the bonds of love and trust that connected them to others.

One passage in the scroll recounted the story of a woman named Fatima, who had been known for her kindness and generosity toward her neighbors. Fatima lived in a small village outside Cordoba, and although she was not wealthy, she was always willing to share what little she had with others. Whether it was preparing food for a neighbor in need or offering a kind word to someone who was struggling, Fatima embodied the spirit of *Ihsan* in her relationships.

The scroll described how Fatima would often recite a verse from the Qur'an that guided her interactions with others:

"And speak to people good [words] and establish prayer and give zakah."

(Qur'an 2:83)

This verse reminded Fatima that kindness, generosity, and good speech were essential components of *Ihsan* in relationships. She believed that by treating others with compassion and respect, she was fulfilling her duty to Allah and contributing to the harmony of her community.

One of the most famous stories about Fatima involved a time when a neighbor had wronged her by spreading false rumors about her family. Instead of responding with anger or seeking revenge, Fatima chose to forgive the neighbor and offer her help when the neighbor fell ill. When asked why she had shown such mercy, Fatima replied:

"Our Prophet taught us that the strong person is not the one who can overpower others, but the one who can control their anger. By showing mercy, I hope that Allah will show mercy to me."

The scroll described Fatima's approach to *Ihsan* in relationships with these words:

"Fatima believed that excellence in relationships was not about being right or seeking justice—it was about embodying mercy, forgiveness, and kindness in every interaction. Through her compassion and generosity, Fatima created a sense of harmony in her community, earning the love and respect of her neighbors and the pleasure of Allah."

This story resonated deeply with Idris. He realized that *Ihsan* in relationships was about more than just being kind—it was about going above and beyond in treating others with mercy, forgiveness, and respect. Fatima had shown him that excellence in relationships was not about seeking perfection, but about striving to be the best version of oneself in every interaction, always seeking to please Allah through one's treatment of others.

Idris was reminded of another verse from the Qur'an that emphasized the importance of kindness and *Ihsan* in relationships:

"And do good as Allah has done good to you. And desire not corruption in the land. Indeed, Allah does not like corrupters."

(Qur'an 28:77)

This verse underscored the idea that believers were called to show kindness and excellence in their interactions with others, just as Allah had shown mercy and generosity to them. For Idris, this meant striving to be patient, forgiving, and compassionate in his relationships, always seeking to improve the bonds of love and trust that connected him to others.

Ihsan in Personal Growth and Self-Discipline

AS IDRIS CONTINUED reading, the scroll explored the role of *Ihsan* in personal growth and self-discipline. The people of Andalusia had understood that excellence was not just about external achievements—it was also about inner development, striving to improve one's character, habits, and relationship with Allah. For them, *Ihsan* in personal growth meant being disciplined in one's actions, constantly seeking to overcome one's weaknesses and to develop the virtues that would bring them closer to Allah.

One passage in the scroll recounted the story of a young man named Khalid, who had struggled with anger and impatience throughout his life. Khalid had always been quick to lose his temper, and his lack of self-control had caused problems in his relationships with his family and friends. But Khalid was determined to improve himself, and he sought the advice of a scholar in Cordoba who had taught him about the importance of *Ihsan* in personal growth.

The scroll described how the scholar had shared a verse from the Qur'an with Khalid that emphasized the importance of self-discipline:

"And those who strive for Us—We will surely guide them to Our ways. And indeed, Allah is with the doers of good (Ihsan)."

(Qur'an 29:69)

This verse reminded Khalid that striving for excellence in personal growth was a lifelong journey, and that Allah would guide him as long as he remained committed to improving himself. The scholar encouraged Khalid to practice patience and self-discipline, reminding him that true excellence was not about perfection, but about the effort to overcome one's weaknesses and to develop the virtues that would bring him closer to Allah.

The scroll described Khalid's journey of personal growth with these words:

"Khalid understood that Ihsan in personal growth was not about being perfect—it was about striving to be better each day, to overcome one's weaknesses, and to develop the virtues that would bring him closer to Allah. Through patience, self-discipline, and constant effort, Khalid transformed his character, becoming a source of calm and wisdom for those around him."

This story inspired Idris to reflect on his own journey of personal growth. He realized that *Ihsan* was not just about achieving external success—it was about developing the inner qualities of patience, humility, and self-discipline that would bring him closer to Allah. Khalid had shown him that excellence in personal growth was a lifelong journey, one that required constant effort and dedication.

Idris was reminded of another hadith of the Prophet Muhammad (PBUH) that emphasized the importance of striving for excellence in personal character:

"The best of you are those who have the best character."

(Sahih Bukhari)

This hadith underscored the idea that *Ihsan* in personal growth was not about external achievements, but about developing the inner qualities that would bring one closer to Allah and improve one's relationships with others.

Reflection: The Power of Ihsan in Bringing One Closer to Allah

AS IDRIS CLOSED THE scroll, he felt a deep sense of inspiration and clarity. The stories of Abdul Malik, Yusuf, Fatima, and Khalid had shown him that *Ihsan* was not just about achieving excellence in specific areas of life—it was about striving for excellence in everything one did, whether in worship, work, relationships, or personal growth.

Idris realized that *Ihsan* was the key to living a life that was deeply connected to Allah. By striving for excellence in every action, believers could transform even the simplest tasks into acts of worship, drawing closer to Allah with every step. The concept of *Ihsan* offered a powerful framework for personal and spiritual growth, encouraging believers to seek Allah's pleasure in everything they did.

One of the verses from the Qur'an that Idris found particularly meaningful as he reflected on these ideas was from *Surah Al-Baqarah*:

"Indeed, Allah loves those who act with excellence (Ihsan)."

(Qur'an 2:195)

This verse reminded Idris that *Ihsan* was not just a goal to be achieved—it was a way of life, a means of earning Allah's love and pleasure. By striving for excellence in every aspect of life, Idris knew that he could bring himself closer to Allah and fulfill his purpose as a servant of the Divine.

As Idris thought about how he could apply these lessons in his own life, he made a commitment to approach every action with *Ihsan*. Whether in his prayers, his work, or his relationships, he would strive to do everything with care, intention, and a sense of responsibility to Allah. He knew that *Ihsan* was not about perfection—it was about the effort to be better each day, to improve oneself, and to seek Allah's pleasure in all things.

Conclusion

In *Chapter 14: The Pursuit of Excellence – Ihsan in All Things*, the protagonist, Idris, learns through the scrolls about the central role of *Ihsan* —excellence—in the lives of Andalusian scholars, craftsmen, and ordinary people. The chapter explores how *Ihsan* was not just a principle that applied to acts of worship, but a way of life that encompassed work, relationships, and personal growth.

The reflection emphasizes that striving for *Ihsan* in all areas of life is a means of drawing closer to Allah and fulfilling one's purpose as a servant of the Divine. The chapter highlights the importance of approaching every action with care, intention, and a sense of responsibility, recognizing that every moment is an opportunity to seek Allah's pleasure and to bring oneself closer to Him.

As Idris reflects on these lessons, he is inspired to make *Ihsan* a guiding principle in his own life, recognizing that by striving for excellence in all things, he can deepen his connection to Allah and transform every aspect of his life into an act of worship. The Qur'anic call to pursue *Ihsan* offers a powerful framework for personal and spiritual growth, encouraging believers to seek excellence in all that they do, and to live lives that are pleasing to Allah.

Chapter 15: The Legacy of Andalusia – Faith for the Future

The final scroll felt heavier in Idris' hands, though it was no different from the others in weight. It wasn't the physical mass of the scroll that gave it gravity—it was the significance of what it represented. As Idris prepared to read the last of the Andalusian scrolls, he realized that this was not just an end, but also a beginning. Through these scrolls, he had been granted access to the wisdom of one of the most vibrant and enduring Islamic civilizations in history. Andalusia's golden age of scholarship, tolerance, and faith had left an indelible mark on the world, and now Idris understood his responsibility to carry this legacy forward.

The scroll before him was not only about the past; it was a guide for the future. It reminded Idris of the profound connection between the lessons of history and the ongoing journey of the Muslim Ummah. As he unrolled the scroll, the first verse that met his eyes encapsulated this sentiment perfectly:

"O you who have believed, if you support Allah, He will support you and plant firmly your feet."

(Qur'an 47:7)

This verse reminded Idris of the importance of maintaining steadfast faith, but it also carried the weight of responsibility. It was not enough to merely reflect on the past—Muslims must actively support the cause of Allah by living and sharing the wisdom of Islam in their daily lives. As he began to read the scroll, Idris felt a deep sense of connection, not just to the scholars and rulers of Andalusia, but to the entire Muslim Ummah, past, present, and future.

The Legacy of Andalusian Scholarship

THE SCROLL BEGAN BY recounting the profound legacy of Andalusian scholarship. During the golden age of Islamic rule in Andalusia, cities like

Cordoba, Seville, and Granada had become centers of learning and culture. Scholars from across the Muslim world and beyond came to study in the libraries and universities of Andalusia, where they engaged in deep theological, scientific, philosophical, and artistic pursuits.

Andalusian scholarship was not limited to Islamic theology—it encompassed a wide range of disciplines, including mathematics, astronomy, medicine, literature, and philosophy. The scholars of Andalusia believed that the pursuit of knowledge was an essential aspect of faith, and they saw no contradiction between reason and revelation. In fact, they believed that the Qur'an encouraged intellectual exploration and discovery, as evidenced by verses like this one:

"Say, 'Are those who know equal to those who do not know?' Only they will remember [who are] people of understanding."

(Qur'an 39:9)

This verse underscored the idea that knowledge was a gift from Allah, and that seeking it was a way of deepening one's understanding of both the world and the Divine. The scholars of Andalusia had taken this principle to heart, dedicating their lives to the pursuit of knowledge and the dissemination of wisdom.

One passage in the scroll recounted the story of Ibn Rushd (Averroes), the famous Andalusian philosopher and jurist who had made significant contributions to both Islamic and Western thought. Ibn Rushd believed that knowledge and faith were deeply interconnected, and he argued that the study of philosophy and science was not only permissible in Islam but also encouraged by the Qur'an.

The scroll described Ibn Rushd's approach to knowledge with these words:

"Ibn Rushd believed that the pursuit of knowledge was a form of worship, a way of understanding the Divine through the study of His creation. He saw no conflict between faith and reason—instead, he believed that reason was a gift from Allah, to be used in the service of faith. Through his works, Ibn Rushd left a legacy of

intellectual rigor and devotion to truth, showing future generations that knowledge was a path to both spiritual and intellectual fulfillment."

This story resonated deeply with Idris. He realized that the scholars of Andalusia had left behind more than just books and ideas—they had left a legacy of intellectual excellence and a deep commitment to seeking truth. Their work had laid the foundation for much of the scientific and philosophical progress that followed, and their influence could still be felt in the modern world.

Idris was reminded of another verse from the Qur'an that emphasized the importance of seeking knowledge and understanding:

"Indeed, in the creation of the heavens and the earth and the alternation of the night and the day are signs for those of understanding."

(Qur'an 3:190)

This verse underscored the idea that the world itself was a source of knowledge and wisdom, and that by studying it, believers could gain a deeper understanding of Allah's creation and their place within it. For Idris, the legacy of Andalusian scholarship was a reminder that the pursuit of knowledge was not just a historical endeavor—it was an ongoing responsibility for all Muslims.

Andalusia as a Model of Coexistence and Unity

AS IDRIS CONTINUED reading, the scroll shifted its focus to one of the most remarkable aspects of Andalusia's legacy—the model of coexistence and unity that had characterized its society. During the golden age of Islamic rule in Andalusia, Muslims, Christians, and Jews had lived and worked together in relative harmony, contributing to a rich cultural and intellectual environment.

This period of convivencia (coexistence) had been a testament to the Qur'anic principles of justice, fairness, and respect for others, regardless of their faith or background. The rulers of Andalusia had understood that the strength of their society lay in its diversity, and they had fostered an environment where people of different religions could collaborate and learn from one another.

One passage in the scroll recounted the story of how Muslims, Christians, and Jews had worked together to build the Great Mosque of Cordoba, one of the most magnificent architectural achievements of the time. The mosque had not only been a place of worship for Muslims but also a symbol of the cultural and intellectual collaboration that defined Andalusian society.

The scroll described the construction of the mosque with these words:

"The Great Mosque of Cordoba stood as a testament to the spirit of unity that permeated Andalusian society. Its construction was not just the work of Muslim architects and builders—Christians and Jews had also contributed their skills and knowledge, working together to create a masterpiece of art and engineering. The mosque became a symbol of the harmony that was possible when people of different faiths worked together for a common purpose."

This story reminded Idris of the importance of unity and cooperation in building strong, just societies. The legacy of Andalusia showed that Muslims had not only been capable of creating a great civilization but had done so by embracing diversity and fostering mutual respect among different religious communities.

Idris was reminded of a verse from the Qur'an that emphasized the importance of justice and fairness in dealing with others:

"O you who have believed, be persistently standing firm in justice, witnesses for Allah, even if it be against yourselves or parents and relatives. Whether one is rich or poor, Allah is more worthy of both."

(Qur'an 4:135)

This verse underscored the idea that justice and fairness were core principles of Islam, and that they applied to all people, regardless of their social or religious status. The rulers and scholars of Andalusia had embodied this principle, creating a society where people of different faiths could live and work together in peace.

For Idris, the legacy of Andalusia's convivencia was a powerful reminder that the Muslim Ummah had a responsibility to promote unity, justice, and mutual respect in the modern world. The lessons of Andalusia were not just historical—they were relevant to the challenges facing the Muslim world today, as believers sought to build societies that were both faithful to Islamic principles and inclusive of others.

The Importance of Preserving Islamic History

AS IDRIS CONTINUED reading, the scroll explored the importance of preserving and sharing the knowledge of Islamic history. The legacy of Andalusia was a reminder of the richness of Islamic civilization and the contributions that Muslims had made to the world in the fields of science, art, philosophy, and governance. But it was also a reminder that this legacy needed to be preserved, studied, and shared with future generations.

One passage in the scroll recounted the story of a group of scholars who had worked tirelessly to preserve the manuscripts and books that had been written during the golden age of Andalusia. As political instability threatened the region, these scholars had risked their lives to save the knowledge that had been accumulated over centuries, ensuring that it would not be lost to history.

The scroll described the efforts of these scholars with these words:

"The scholars of Andalusia understood that knowledge was a trust from Allah, and that it was their responsibility to preserve it for future generations. As their libraries were threatened with destruction, they worked day and night to copy and protect the manuscripts that contained the wisdom of their civilization. Through their efforts, the legacy of Andalusia was preserved, allowing future generations to learn from the past and build upon its achievements."

This story inspired Idris to reflect on the importance of preserving Islamic history in the modern world. He realized that the knowledge and wisdom of past Islamic civilizations, like Andalusia, were not just relics of the past—they were sources of guidance and inspiration for the future. But in order to benefit from this legacy, it was essential to preserve and share it.

Idris was reminded of a hadith of the Prophet Muhammad (PBUH) that emphasized the importance of seeking and preserving knowledge:

"The seeking of knowledge is obligatory for every Muslim."

(Ibn Majah)

This hadith underscored the idea that the pursuit of knowledge was not just a personal responsibility—it was a collective obligation for the entire Muslim Ummah. By preserving the knowledge of the past, Muslims could ensure that future generations would have access to the wisdom and guidance needed to navigate the challenges of their time.

For Idris, this meant not only studying Islamic history himself but also sharing it with others. He realized that the lessons of Andalusia were not just for scholars or historians—they were for everyone. By learning from the past, Muslims could build a future that was rooted in the principles of justice, knowledge, and faith.

Faith for the Future: Applying the Lessons of Andalusia

AS IDRIS REACHED THE final section of the scroll, he felt a deep sense of responsibility. The legacy of Andalusia had taught him profound lessons about faith, knowledge, justice, and unity. But these lessons were not meant to remain in the past—they were meant to be applied in the present and the future.

The scroll ended with a reflection on the importance of carrying the legacy of Andalusia forward:

"The legacy of Andalusia is not just a story of the past—it is a guide for the future. The lessons of knowledge, justice, and unity that were practiced in Andalusia are as relevant today as they were centuries ago. It is the responsibility of every believer to preserve this legacy and to apply its wisdom in their own lives, ensuring that the light of Islam continues to shine for future generations."

This reflection struck Idris deeply. He realized that the wisdom he had gained from the Andalusian scrolls was not just for his own personal growth—it was a trust that he was now responsible for sharing with others. The lessons of Andalusia were timeless, and they offered solutions to many of the challenges facing the Muslim Ummah today.

Idris was reminded of a verse from the Qur'an that emphasized the importance of working for the future:

"And prepare for them whatever you are able of power and of steeds of war by which you may terrify the enemy of Allah and your enemy and others besides them whom you do not know [but] whom Allah knows. And whatever you spend in the cause of Allah will be fully repaid to you, and you will not be wronged."

(Qur'an 8:60)

This verse reminded Idris that Muslims were called to prepare for the future, not only in terms of physical strength but also in terms of intellectual and spiritual preparation. The knowledge and wisdom of the past were essential tools for building a future that was strong, just, and faithful to the principles of Islam.

As Idris reflected on how he could apply the lessons of Andalusia in his own life, he made a commitment to live by the principles of *Ihsan*, justice, and unity that had defined the golden age of Andalusian civilization. He would strive for excellence in his worship, his work, and his relationships, always seeking to deepen his connection to Allah and to serve the Muslim Ummah.

But Idris also understood that this was not a journey he could undertake alone. He realized that the legacy of Andalusia was a collective inheritance, one that needed to be shared and preserved by the entire Muslim Ummah. By working together, Muslims could ensure that the wisdom of the past would continue to guide and inspire future generations.

Reflection: Shaping the Future of the Muslim Ummah

AS IDRIS CLOSED THE final scroll, he felt a deep sense of connection to the past, but also a renewed sense of purpose for the future. The legacy of Andalusia had taught him that the Muslim Ummah was capable of great achievements when it remained faithful to the principles of knowledge, justice, and unity. But it had also reminded him that these achievements were not guaranteed—they required ongoing effort, dedication, and a commitment to preserving the wisdom of the past.

Idris realized that the lessons of Andalusia could shape the future of the Muslim Ummah in profound ways. By studying and applying the principles of knowledge, justice, and unity that had defined Andalusian society, Muslims could build communities that were strong, just, and inclusive. But in order to do this, it was essential to preserve and share the knowledge of Islamic history, ensuring that future generations would have access to the wisdom and guidance needed to navigate the challenges of their time.

One of the verses from the Qur'an that Idris found particularly meaningful as he reflected on these ideas was from *Surah Al-Hadid*:

"Has the time not come for those who have believed that their hearts should become humbly submissive at the remembrance of Allah and what has come down of the truth?"

(Qur'an 57:16)

This verse reminded Idris that the time to act was now. The legacy of Andalusia had shown him the path forward, but it was up to him and the rest of the Muslim Ummah to walk that path with humility, dedication, and a deep sense of responsibility to Allah.

As Idris thought about how he could contribute to shaping the future of the Muslim Ummah, he made a commitment to share the lessons of Andalusia with others. He would not only study and apply the wisdom he had gained from the scrolls—he would also work to preserve and share this knowledge, ensuring that the legacy of Andalusia would continue to inspire future generations.

Conclusion

In *Chapter 15: The Legacy of Andalusia – Faith for the Future*, the protagonist, Idris, reflects on the enduring legacy of Andalusia and the profound lessons he has learned from the scrolls. The chapter explores how the knowledge and wisdom of Andalusian scholars, rulers, and communities can shape the future of the Muslim Ummah, offering guidance on how to build strong, just, and inclusive societies.

The reflection emphasizes the importance of preserving and sharing the knowledge of Islamic history, recognizing that the lessons of the past are essential tools for navigating the challenges of the present and future. The chapter highlights the role of *Ihsan*, justice, and unity in building a future that is faithful to the principles of Islam, and it calls on the Muslim Ummah to work together to preserve and apply the wisdom of the past.

As Idris reflects on these lessons, he is inspired to make a commitment to sharing the knowledge he has gained from the Andalusian scrolls, recognizing that the legacy of Andalusia is a trust that must be preserved for future generations. The Qur'anic call to seek knowledge, promote justice, and work for the future offers a powerful framework for shaping the future of the Muslim Ummah, ensuring that the light of Islam continues to shine for generations to come.

Don't miss out!

Visit the website below and you can sign up to receive emails whenever Amina Zahra publishes a new book. There's no charge and no obligation.

https://books2read.com/r/B-A-CCQYC-ISAKF

BOOKS2READ

Connecting independent readers to independent writers.

About the Author

Amina Zahra is an award-winning Young Adult fiction writer who explores themes of spirituality, identity, and cultural heritage. Growing up in Istanbul, she witnessed the beauty and challenges of blending tradition with modernity, which inspires her storytelling. Amina is passionate about creating characters that reflect the diverse experiences of Muslim teens and often hosts workshops to encourage young writers to share their unique voices.